DANGEROUS GAME

BLACK CIPHER FILES #4

LISA HUGHEY

LISA HUGHEY

DANGEROUS GAME

by

Lisa Hughey

Copyright April 2016

Lisa Hughey

Ebook ISBN: 978-0-9964352-5-3

Paperback ISBN: 978-1-950359-05-9

Hardback ISBN: 978-1-950359-17-2

 Created with Vellum

To fans of Yippee ki-yay motherfucker

CHAPTER 1

I've been in love with the same guy for five years.

Unfortunately, he found someone else. At first I was... upset. But once I observed Lucas Goodman with his new friend —yeah, you couldn't really call Jamie Hunt a girl, more like a badass—I knew my chances were over.

Every time I was in their presence, I felt the loss of our relationship keenly. Sexual tension and sheer attraction vibrated between Lucas and Jamie like a nearly visible arc.

They fit. In a way Lucas and I never had.

I've been lucky. I traveled for my job. A lot. I've seen many places in the world. I dined in five-star restaurants and slumbered in five-star hotels. I have my own French-style country villa with a few acres of wine grapes for a backyard.

My job was fascinating. My friends plentiful. My options varied.

And I was bored out of my mind. At thirty-four years old, lately I found I was a little lost. I'd really like someone to share an adventure with me.

That was how I found myself standing in line at the South

Korean Ambassador's residence in Washington, DC on a blind date. Set up by none other than my former lover, Lucas, and his, umm, badass girlfriend, friend, whatever.

At least, I thought it was a date. With Lucas and Jamie I could never tell. It was possible they needed my help on some top-secret super-spy experiment.

Except, who was I kidding? They might involve me if there was some scientific analysis or even a situation that required rudimentary medical knowledge, but I hardly thought my date was going to need me for anything other than, well, a date.

Ken Park, the date, smiled blandly.

He was gorgeous. He had that strong Korean jawline, sculpted cheekbones with smooth and tight skin—that on someone like me would look fake or like I'd had serious work done—and a high forehead.

A thick hank of shiny black hair fell over his right eyebrow in a studied casualness, while the rest of his head was shaved and manscaped to perfection, all clean lines and military-precise sharp edges. I wasn't sure his mental acuity extended past looking good. Like he'd expended all his capacity gelling his hair into those sharp lines, his gaze held a bland vacancy. He seemed far too young for the amount of medals spanning his fairly broad chest.

He was not my type. At all.

I preferred men who looked like men.

A little scruffy and muscular. Yes, that made me shallow. And yeah, I was pretty sure he had some muscles underneath his military uniform—his shoulders were definitely wide, but his ass was smaller than mine.

For some indefinable reason, he rubbed me the wrong way, like a burr in the heel of a running shoe. I was uncomfortable in my skin. Itchy, twitchy. I didn't think he liked me much either.

Except, *except*, I was oddly attracted to him. Mental capacity aside, he emitted pheromones that made my body sit up and beg.

My hormones were going haywire. We'd been mostly silent while we waited in the security line.

"So…Ken." What the hell did I say now. "How do you know Ja—" Shit, I almost messed up and said Jamie. "Janine?"

Did I mention that Lucas was dating a spy? He'd never come out and admitted it but I put two and two together and came up with sixty-four. Especially since she mentioned on the phone when she was setting me up that my date knew her as Janine.

His mouth quirked, and I thought maybe there was more under that pretty boy exterior than a sub-par IQ. "We used to date."

Seriously? I was on a date with one of Jamie Hunt's castoffs?

What the hell did I do in a former life to deserve this?

Okay. I needed to let that go. I was determined to relish this experience, if not my date.

Time to focus on the positives. I was going to an embassy party. I'd never been to a diplomatic event and one of the things I'd resolved to do this year was to try new adventures.

My life had become predictable and boring.

He leaned closer, and a shiver cascaded over my spine as he whispered in my ear, "How do you know Janine?" Was it my imagination or did he hesitate over Jamie's cover name?

A strange sort of heat shimmered over my skin as his lips brushed my ear. And a trickle—okay, a flood—of awareness invaded my senses. How could I be attracted to this guy?

"Ah, mutual friend."

He nodded and eased away from me. Suddenly I had the sense that he'd crowded my personal space on purpose, as if he had no intention of being dismissed. Which based on my interpretation of his intelligence didn't seem right.

But whatever I thought I'd seen lurking behind his open gaze disappeared and his face was once again that bland, vacuous mask.

"What brings you to DC?" he asked.

3

"A conference." Nothing he'd understand based on the way his eyes had glazed when I told him earlier that my specialty was molecular biology. And yet I couldn't shake the idea that he was playing me.

"How nice." But he clearly meant *how boring*.

He might be right on that one.

Ken glanced around, his gaze skimming the security at the entrance. And I couldn't say why, but I thought he was unhappy. "Everything okay?"

"Of course," he answered smoothly. But he was lying through his pretty white smile. His tension was visible in the very relaxed lines of his body. He wasn't happy right now. Somehow I seemed to be the only one who'd picked up on the disparity between his unperturbed posture and his internal tension.

He carefully assessed the guards stationed at the door. His attention lingered on the guard's gun.

"Mmm, don't think so."

He shrugged elegantly, a lift of his shoulder, nothing more. "I thought there would be more guards."

"With guns?"

He inclined his head but his attention was clearly not on me.

I shuddered. "I hate guns."

"They are necessary in a violent world," Ken replied carefully. Almost as if he were reciting a line rather than something he believed. "The Republic of Korea has many enemies."

True. "But what are the odds that those enemies would be here this afternoon?" I said tightly. I mean really. We were in Washington DC. He was military; clearly guns were a way of life for him. Likely he wore one as an extension of his dick rather than an instrument of defense.

A predatory look entered his eyes. "One must always be prepared for war."

Fortunately, I'd never seen the damage a gun could do up

4

close. A ghost of foreboding shivered over my spine. "Give me a nice biological weapon any day."

"Ah, but the potential for disaster is much greater," Ken replied. "I would not have pegged you as quite so bloodthirsty."

Really, he'd actually tried to stereotype *me*?

This date was going downhill fast.

PERFECT. Ken Park mentally rolled his eyes. Who the hell had Jamie stuck him with? Barbara Williams seemed to be a cerebral snob and so absolutely not his type. She'd been so busy making assumptions that she completely missed his ability to do more than form a sentence. Which was irrelevant, and yet he was still pissed. He was tempted to dump her before they got to the receiving line. Unfortunately, he needed her.

Intellectually, Barb was a complete turnoff. Too bad his dick hadn't gotten the message. He thought she was *fine*. She was messing with his concentration and not in a good way.

DC was experiencing an unseasonably warm spring, and Barb had forgone an outer coat. With her coffee-and-cream skin exposed by the shimmering beaded dress, she had the perfect form for his dick to find some excitement.

The drape of her dress revealed the sinuous lines of her back and dipped low, drawing the attention to her absolutely gorgeous rounded ass.

And he needed to get his focus back where it belonged. On this mission. He'd been preparing his whole life for this opportunity. He couldn't blow it now because of a piece of ass, even if it was exquisite.

They finally made it to the entrance. The embassy party, being held at the ambassador's residence rather than the embassy on Massachusetts Avenue, was awfully light on guards. The alternate location was an unusual choice but it was also the reason he had gotten this opportunity tonight.

The lack of security would make his mission easier, fewer people to evade, and yet a subtle unease hovered. Why had Ambassador Choi chosen today to reduce his security staff?

The entrance portico was protected by a temporary canvas popup tent that would shield the entering guests from rain or drone surveillance.

"Invitation, *ju-seyo*," the guard said.

"Ken Park, the Franklin Group, former ROKA, and his companion for the evening." Ken executed a half bow and nod at the security detail and handed the guard the fifty-pound cream invitation engraved with his name and position and the ambassador's seal of The Republic of Korea.

Officially he worked for the lobbyist branch of the Franklin Group, a foreign policy think tank. His familiarity with US politics and South Korean military made him attractive as a lobbyist. After he'd resigned his Korean army commission several years ago, he moved back to the US. The South Koreans believed he was passing them information.

The US knew he was passing information to his birth country. In fact, they facilitated the passing. When he was in the ROK Army he'd passed information to the US.

"*Kamsahamnida.*" The guard welcomed them, and bowed low in the traditional gesture of respect. Ken outranked the soldier by several pay grades.

"Surrender your cell phones, *ju-seyo*."

Ken had planned ahead for this. "Left them in our vehicle." No way was he letting embassy employees get a look at his cell, even if it was encrypted and the security detail shouldn't have enough time or expertise to break it.

The guard made a note on their invitation.

"Oh," Barb reached for it.

The guard frowned at her.

Jen-jang. Ken could not let her keep that invite. The micro-thin listening patch he'd affixed to the back cost an emperor's fortune. He needed that device to end up inside the ambassador's home office.

That had been the price of the intel he'd acquired for today's mission.

"Is it possible to keep the invitation?" Barb asked. He swore to God, she was practically batting her thick black lashes at the young sentry.

"Sorry, ma'am."

"Oh." She actually seemed disappointed.

"What did you want the invitation for?" Ken held her arm as he led her through the ornate two-story doors and into the foyer of the ambassador's home. Maybe he needed to reassess her. Was it possible she was a plant? He'd trusted Jamie. Perhaps he'd been wrong to do so.

"Memento."

Certainly not of this date, he thought derisively. "For what?"

"Scrapbook," Barb replied dryly. "Surely your mother kept little tokens to remind her of special events."

Yeah. When she was facilitating the escape of her family of five from Gwangju and evading the Korean army, she decided to carry a few party invites in their single suitcase. "She wasn't much for souvenirs."

"Why did Janice recommend me?" Barb blurted out.

"I needed a——" *decoy,* "—date."

She certainly was a stunning decoy. Ken skimmed his appreciative gaze over her assets. The glittering dress with bronze beading accented her lustrous mocha skin. Her short black hair, which he hated on women, feathered against her cheeks and arrowed to a full, luxurious mouth slicked with a shimmering bronze that matched her dress. Her striking deep brown eyes had a slightly exotic tilt and her eyelids sparkled with bronze shadow.

Everything about her screamed *sophistication.*

No one would be paying any attention to him; their focus would be on her. Perfect. Decoy.

Barb snorted, the gesture so absolutely inelegant that he was charmed. That certainly wasn't a scripted response. "I'd think a guy like you could get your own date."

"A guy like me?" He raised one eyebrow, as his mind worked feverishly.

Because clearly she wasn't an asset. And clearly she wasn't a spy. She spoke far too directly for either job. He'd halfway assumed that Jamie would set him up with someone to watch him.

Ken found her directness oddly...refreshing.

"Handsome," she sneered. Looks apparently weren't important to her since she was openly dismissing him. He'd used his pretty-boy face to excellent effect to distract his enemies and adversaries on more than one occasion.

"Muscular."

Now he knew she was lying. He purposely chose suits just a little too big in order to hide the fact that he was very physically fit. His muscles were camouflaged beneath the ill-fitting disguise. It was the Korean way to understate your attributes and conceal your strength from your opponent.

If anything he appeared slightly frail beneath the loose suit.

For whatever bizarre reason, her dismissal and obvious disdain stung.

He wanted to remove his coat, flex his muscles, show her just how muscular he really was, which was anathema to his normal habits. He liked it when people underestimated him.

Barb continued listing his attributes, except her tone indicated she considered them more negatives than positives.

So when she said "Well...." he couldn't resist taunting: "Hung?"

The need to unsettle her, to rattle her, was uncommon and

unexpected. Trained operatives couldn't get him to break his cover personality. And she'd done it without even trying.

A flush worked over her face, and her brown eyes sparkled with temper, even as her gaze dropped instinctively to his crotch.

"I was going to say *connected*." Tension made her voice husky.

Now he knew she was thinking about his dick. Which was far better than her thinking about why she was here with him. She definitely wasn't stupid.

He'd shown his hand by giving in to the desire to let her know that he was more than just a pretty face. Poor strategy on his part. Except he shouldn't need strategy with her, she was nothing more than a simple pawn on this op.

But, oh, was he going to pay Jamie Hunt back for this.

CHAPTER 2

J amie Hunt was going to owe me. I can't believe I had been
excited about this date.

While Ken's expression was pleasant, almost vacuous, I
sensed he was pissed. Even though there was nothing in the light
clasp of his hand that indicated he was annoyed.

Inside the vaulted foyer, we paused to remove our shoes. A
shoe attendant gave Ken a retrieval card, and I gave a little
prayer of thanks that I'd gotten a pedicure before coming to DC.

"It is customary to remove the shoes in a traditional Korean
home." Ken sounded like a tour guide. "Many people both eat
and sleep on the floor, which necessitates a clean living area."

He led me through intricately carved wood doors. "This door
is an example of a *Soseulbitkkotsalmun* carving. The cherry
blossoms represent the confluence and harmony of Korean and
US interests, emphasizing our similarities rather than our
differences."

He escorted me into the main party room.

The design was a mix of traditional Korean furnishings and
Western décor. There were low wood plank tables that appeared

to be very old surrounded by embroidered sitting cushions and interspersed with taller Western-style mahogany tables with standard chairs.

Intricately carved, wood-paneled sliding "walls" had opened smaller rooms to create one large gathering area.

Female servers were attired in a mashup of a *hanbok*, traditional Korean dress, and modern US fashion. They wore strapless sage green dresses with a band beneath the breasts and a fluffy puff of skirt that hit at mid-thigh, and ornamented with pink sash. Carrying trays of gorgeously constructed foods artfully displayed on discs of a marbled wood, they moved through the room with a graceful elegance.

Because I was an information junkie, I tallied up the aphrodisiac qualities of the platters, a smorgasbord of salmon, almonds, ginseng, figs, eggs, avocado, saffron, all foods purported to increase sexual drive. Was that on purpose?

My date—I was using that term loosely—seemed to be waiting for something. I could sense the anticipation simmering beneath his calm, disinterested demeanor. He was on edge, with a subtle expectancy. I just had no idea *what* he was waiting for.

I had to revise my original opinion that he was just a pretty face. I now believed he hid his cunning beneath a simple, handsome exterior.

Since we entered the large party room, he'd gushed over a collection of celadon ceramic sculptures artfully displayed on plain wood rectangular pedestals; a trio of *pojagi*, traditional Korean wrapping cloth; and copper urns filled with cherry blossom branches.

"The ambassador's younger brother is a dealer in fine Korean art. Although I've never met him, they're both reputed to have a collector's appreciation for antiquities and preserving our heritage," Ken droned on.

If he truly had interest in any of those things, I'd eat my La

Perla strapless silk bra with the Spanish scalloped lace. He absolutely knew his collectibles but he wasn't into it. At all.

"The architecture of this house is beautiful. What is the design called?" I simulated an interested smile.

"This is a traditional Korean home called a *hanok*."

Ken had split his attention between me, who was clearly starting to get on his nerves—why that fact gave me immeasurable pleasure I couldn't say—and the ancient *pojagi* hanging above a doorway.

"Traditional *hanok* architecture uses nature's bounty and recyclable materials, which is why you see an abundance of slate flooring and the natural wood accents, as well as the simple oiled paper, or *hanji*, in the panels of the doors. Even the roof—" he gestured to the floor to ceiling windows that revealed an open courtyard garden, "—is made from a natural clay."

As Ken espoused the qualities of traditional Korean design, he held one of my hands in his, running his finger along my forearm in a simple yet effective embrace. Even knowing I was being played, and likely used as a distraction, I couldn't help the shiver at his easy, absent-minded caress.

Because if I wasn't mistaken, not only was he using me as a distraction, he was trying to distract me as well.

The diversion I presented to the other guests was obvious. I was the only African-American woman in the room and so I garnered a decent amount of attention. Which I could deal with but I wanted to know why it was so important to have eyes on me and not on my date.

Even without my heels on, I was nearly a head taller than most of the women present.

I stood out spectacularly.

I'd been set up. At this point, I didn't know who to blame. Jamie or Ken?

"Kenneth, introduce me to your date." A distinguished-looking older gentleman with a head full of silver hair and the ruddy face of a man acquainted with a scotch bottle slapped Ken on the back.

"Dick." He executed a short bow.

For a minute, I thought he was calling the man a dick.

"Nice to see you." Ken held out his hand the two men shook. With far more enthusiasm than he'd shown up to this point, Ken introduced me to his boss, Dick Herring of the Franklin Group.

The older man grasped my fingers and bowed low over my hand. "Enchanted."

The gesture was old-fashioned and should have been an affectation but somehow he pulled it off.

"Let's both enjoy the rare evening off," Dick said. "However, if you have a chance to set up a meeting with Kim, get it done."

Ken nodded.

"A pleasure." Dick smiled, his blue eyes twinkling with mirth. "Make sure he shows you a good time. He doesn't get out enough."

I could sense Ken's rising irritation. But he smiled as if he agreed. "Thanks, Dick." That time I definitely heard the edge in his voice.

And because I could tell he was annoyed, I decided to push. "So…" I swirled a finger in my drink, a cherry blossom martini. "Who's Kim?"

"A possible influencer." He neglected to mention what the guy could influence.

"What is it you do?"

"I work for a lobbyist. I'm a liaison between the South Korean government and the US Congress."

I raised a brow.

"It's a way for me to support both my home country and my adopted country, to facilitate positive relations and trade between our great nations."

Facilitate. Big words now. Then I knew that my original assumption had been wrong.

A stately Korean man clapped his hands discreetly, and the conversation around us slowly died. "On behalf of Ambassador Choi, I thank you for coming to witness this historic occasion."

My gaze shot to my date.

He was busy seemingly admiring the hand-stitched textile behind the speaker's head but I could tell that his true attention was elsewhere, as if he were just biding time.

"Please turn your attention to the monitors."

Even the wait staff had stopped what they were doing. Speakers amplified the ceremony on the television screens, where the President of the United States was speaking in front of the Smithsonian, commending the South Koreans on their historic arrangement.

Ambassador Choi stood next to the president. "In a joint exhibit between The Republic of Korea and the United States, we have come together to share treasures that have been presumed lost since the Korean War, or Six-Two-Five. Before being returned to their rightful country, the Republic of Korea, the antiquities will be exhibited at the Smithsonian."

"The international implications for collaboration and unity to restore these treasures to the Republic of Korea represent a clear and continuing step in our quest to strengthen relations between our two countries. This is the type of joint endeavor we need to foster. Working together to find solutions that will benefit both countries. Everyone wins." The president smiled broadly.

Ambassador Choi then spoke to the assembled crowd. "I have worked for years, negotiating with private American collectors to restore these artifacts to my beloved country."

I studied the ambassador on the television. On the wall near the monitor was a formal portrait of the ambassador and his family. The man on the screen had clearly gained weight, his features slightly puffy.

Ambassador Choi bowed to the president. "The Republic of Korea is most grateful to the United States."

The Ambassador's wife pasted a pleasant smile on her face and bowed to the room. "My husband will be arriving from the ceremony as soon as traffic permits. Please enjoy our hospitality. I know he is anxious to celebrate with you all."

The inhabitants of the room clapped enthusiastically. Excited murmurs and a buzz of energy electrified the room. My official date was also clapping but his look was assessing rather than happy.

Somehow I didn't think that anyone else saw beneath his surface. Which was crazy. But I noticed in his interactions with the other party attendees that he played the brainless airhead with sophistication and polish, so he fit in, but didn't blend. Several people had treated him in a condescending manner as if he were a few elements short of a full periodic table. Not overtly, but with a very subtle disrespect that was starting to piss me off.

"Why do people call you different names?"

"My Korean name is Park DaeGuen but that is difficult to pronounce for some. The Americanized version is Ken Park."

"DaeGuen," I said with decent pronunciation.

He paused in his circuit, stared at me.

"I live in California, you know." *Don't fucking dismiss me.* "We have a significant Asian population."

"Point taken." His gaze continued to roam the room, presumably looking for people to connect with.

"Which do you prefer?"

He jolted. "I don't know that it matters. I am a product of both countries."

Something in his voice caught my notice. Finally, my date was getting interesting.

As we circled the edges of the room, Ken's tension rose. It was starting to make me curious.

I'd recognized at least two senators and the current Secretary of Education. Ken seemed to know a lot of people. He worked the room, air-kissing socialites and Korean elites and shaking the hands of the dignitaries in the room.

After about half an hour, I blurted, "It's a who's who of Washington."

"The project has long-term implications for the diplomatic relationship between the US and the Republic of Korea," Ken replied. "We must strengthen our alliance on all levels, not just at the military and political level."

I blinked. This house was filled with people who had major influence in American politics. Powerful. Influential. Connected.

I was so far out of my league that I knew there was more going on than met the eye. And while meeting some of Washington's elite movers and shakers was definitely a tick on my personal bucket list, I didn't like where my mind had gone.

Like an extra pair of chromosomes randomly stuck in the helix, I didn't belong. "What the hell am I doing here?" I whispered.

"You're doing great, *chagiya*," Ken said absently.

Suddenly I'd had enough. This wasn't a date. I wasn't his *chagiya*, whatever that meant. I was his pawn. And I was tired of being used. "Look leave me out of your super-secret…stuff," I hissed, remembering at the last minute to leave out *spy*.

Ken moved closer, crowding my personal space until he was practically plastered against me. He shot me a simmering look so full of dark sexual energy that it could not be misinterpreted. Except with his back to the room, no one could see it but me. "Not now."

Some time ago I'd been on the fringes of an investigation that had put Lucas in the line of fire. I'd helped to decipher the science behind a massive cover-up by the federal government. Of course no one but me and a handful of agents knew about the cover-up or the fact that I'd helped, but still I felt an enormous amount of pride about my role in the investigation.

"Unless you're going to include me whatever you're doing, I

don't appreciate being used." I spoke in a low tone, my mouth at his ear, pretending to whisper sweet nothings to him when what I really wanted was to kick him in the balls.

"I don't know what you're talking about." Ken stepped back, his body relaxing as he glanced around the room. Almost as if he'd forgotten where he was for a second.

"Save it." I wanted to stomp away but I resisted the urge to display my temper. Instead I resolved to swing my hips in a seriously sexy sway. "I'll be in the ladies'."

Once I got my hands on Jamie Hunt I was going to give her a very explicit piece of my mind. I refused to acknowledge the hurt that simmered beneath my anger.

I thought Jamie and I were becoming friends. Instead, I was going to let her know that I did not appreciate being blindsided by subterfuge.

And, I just might try and kick her ass like I'd promised the first time we met.

CHAPTER 3

K en inhaled deeply, his lungs singed with hot woman and even hotter thoughts. Holy shit. As he watched her swing her ass in the age-old female message of "you can look all you want but you will never touch"—and man did he want to touch —his visceral reaction bordered on extreme.

Women were an enjoyable side treat, a morsel to be enjoyed during downtime, or a weapon to be used, or a decoy to misdirect, but he never let one distract him from his mission. His drive. His reason for everything he did. Ever.

He should be trying to do damage control from her insight that this was more than just a simple date to an embassy party. Trying to deflect, to charm, to disarm. Instead he followed her into the bathroom, to calm her down, to discuss this further, not to make good on the heat that combusted between them. Even if that was what his body was screaming for him to do.

"Listen." He needed to placate her but his instinct was to crowd her up against the powder room door and take her mouth. She couldn't yell at him if he was kissing her.

As an excuse it totally worked for him.

"Why am I really here?" she snarled. "And don't fucking lie."

"I needed a—" he tread carefully, "—distracting date."

"Great." She thunked her head back against the door carved in a traditional Korean hexagonal pattern that represented longevity and prosperity. "Six years busting my ass at Stanford and Tufts, a PhD in molecular biology, and years of discrimination for not only being a woman, but a woman of color in a male-dominated field—I had to work harder, prove myself smarter every single fucking day—and the reason I'm here is to be a pretty face."

Jen-jang. "Not just a pretty face. A fucking gorgeous face. And you're messing with my concentration." That was the part he didn't get. She was making him lose his focus. On one of the most important nights of his life, he couldn't concentrate. It was…bewildering.

Ken invaded her personal space, a completely unprofessional move. He had a more pressing directive to leave the main party room, and he should be focused on that mission. He'd been chasing this information for many years.

But for a moment, his parameters changed. He had to taste her.

Had to see if her scent, a blend of violets and citrus, which had been driving him wild since he'd picked her up at the Sofitel on 15th, would explode on his tongue. He caged her between his arms and pressed so closely, he could see the gold flecks in her deep brown eyes and the rim of pure black that circled her irises.

"What are you doing?"

Her lips trembled and her eyelids drooped, her body poised on the edge. And he knew he had a green light. She was as turned on as he was. "Giving what you want." And fuck, what he wanted too.

"You're cra—"

Ken nipped at her mouth and then lunged.

"—oomph."

19

He might have backed off if she hadn't moaned into the carnal kiss and curled her fingers around his biceps. After a tense few seconds, Barb relaxed languidly against the sliding door. Her hips canted toward his, and all the blood in his body rushed to his hardening erection.

Ken curved over her until his chest rubbed against hers. The sword of his cock pressed against her mound as the kiss devolved into a full-body-contact embrace. He angled his head and plundered.

He dragged his tongue along the curve of her jaw and down her neck, and dropped biting kisses against her silky skin. Barb surrendered to his conquering kisses.

"Lord have mercy." She sucked the sensitive skin behind his earlobe.

Ken rocked in a slow, erotic rhythm, as they danced together and then apart in a sensual waltz.

A long tremor sizzled through her and into him. Then the boom of his heart was replaced by another more ominous boom.

Jen-jang. That sounded like a breaching charge.

Ken broke away from Barb.

"What was that?" Her chest was heaving and her hair had a well-sexed look. For half a second he wanted to dive back in and ignore what sounded like World War III as another series of detonations reverberated outside the bathroom door.

"Nothing good." Ken opened the sliding door just enough to peer into the hallway.

The disturbing *rat-a-tat-tat* of automatic weapon fire blasted their ears. Screams and shouts were shrill in the violence-laden air.

"Shit." Ken did one more recon of the hallway and grabbed her hand.

He couldn't afford to be found. At least not before he completed his mission. And he couldn't leave her here.

He did not need this now. The fact that weapons were being

fired at an embassy party was not a good sign. *Understatement of the century.*

"What are you doing?" Barb interrupted his mental tangent.

"We have to get the hell out or we're going to be trapped." He didn't have time to worry about what was going on in the main rooms of the house.

Ken dragged her toward the hidden door in the middle of the hallway. It appeared to be a decorative shield for a window but he knew better. Based on the thunder of boots on the wood parquet floor, they only had seconds.

"Oh, because that's going to stop a bullet," she snarled. Fortunately, whoever had invaded Ambassador Choi's residence was shouting, people were screaming, and rounds were flying because otherwise, she would have given away their position.

Shit. Times two.

"Yell at me later." Ken slid the door to the right and revealed a flat metal square. He flipped the lid and exposed a numeric keypad. He certainly hoped the intel he'd spent years scheming to get worked. They had to get the hell off this floor and out of the line of fire *now.*

He quickly entered the twelve digit code.

"You know about a secret hiding place in the Korean ambassador's home." Sadly, she didn't sound impressed, she sounded pissed. "Distracting date, my ass. I'm a fucking decoy. I'm going to seriously kill Jamie."

"Get in line, *yobo.*" Fuck.

As soon as the hidden elevator door opened wide enough for their bodies to get through, Ken thrust Barb inside. He slammed the wood and paper panel closed and breathed a quick sigh of relief. They weren't out of the woods yet but they'd been granted a slight reprieve.

"Pretty sure I asked for someone who'd be in awe of the guests and the venue," he muttered as he hastily punched the code into the security alarm panel in the elevator. "Not someone who questions every fucking move I make."

The pound of the intruders' boots was nearly deafening. And fuck him, hopefully the automatic elevator door would slide closed before whoever was shooting the hell out of the ambassador's house got to this particular hallway.

Jamie was supposed to set him up with someone who wouldn't ask questions, who would be good arm candy, and who'd distract the other guests while he broke into the super-secret room beneath Ambassador Choi's residence and protected by military-grade encryption measures. Instead he had Barb, who even when things were fucked six ways to Sunday, wanted to argue every fricking thing to death.

Once the metal door slid closed, the lights came on. She closed her mouth but her expressive brown eyes opened even wider. They were in a small elevator, barely four by two. It could accommodate three people standing shoulder to shoulder, maybe four if they really squished inside.

Ken knew from his intelligence that the walls were impenetrable, made from a titanium alloy, and that the cables and box could withstand pressure from a bomb. Which was all well and good, but if the bad guys had the code to get inside, they were screwed.

The lift wouldn't move until Ken entered the command. Right now they needed to stay perfectly still. He couldn't afford for the soldiers to hear the hydraulics. Who knew what other kind of firepower they had.

The terrorists clomping through the residence shook the wall beside their head. Ken pressed a button and the bank of television monitors embedded in the wall flared to life. Six heavily muscled and even more heavily armed men filed through the hallway side by side, weapons up and pointed toward the walls.

Whoever they were, they were carrying DaeWoo standard

military-issue assault rifles, typically used by the ROK Army. And if he wasn't mistaken, the full-body armor they were wearing was state-of-the-art and extremely expensive. So expensive it was prohibitive. A million US dollars for one custom-fitted suit kept most buyers away.

Which meant these guys had excellent intelligence and were extremely well funded.

"Drop," he whispered. "Quietly." The terror on her face struck a chord of remorse. "This elevator is supposed to be soundproofed, but let's not make any assumptions. And I don't know about the shaft. If they hear us, they'll shoot." He spoke calmly, hoping his low-energy level would bring the panic flaring in her eyes down a notch.

Jen-jang.

They slipped to the floor. Quietly. Carefully. Ken placed his body between Barb and the closed elevator doors. He wrapped his arms around her as she tucked her head into the curve of his neck so he could face the bank of monitors and follow what was happening outside their safe haven.

"Embassy party was on my bucket list," she muttered. Her breath puffed against his skin. "Hiding from terrorists was not."

Ken held in his laughter. Now was not the time for humor. But it was hard to remember that with her lush body pressed up against his and the liter of adrenaline punching through his system.

He brushed a light kiss over her forehead, then got to work.

He needed to figure out who had just invaded the South Koreans. Technically, this home was considered South Korean soil. Someone was creating an international incident of epic proportions. While it wasn't his primary directive, Ken wanted to know who he was dealing with. He studied their body language since he couldn't see their faces.

Who the hell were these people and what did they want?

Based on their movements, they were either Korean or Russian trained.

They kicked in the bathroom door and swept for people. They didn't leave any door or closet unsearched. The intruders yanked a man out of the men's room. The guy had his shirt tails out and his pants still undone, and his knees were wet. A thin trickle of blood ran from the man's forehead down into the collar of his white formal shirt. The soldier shoved him forward. The man stumbled, shaking in fear.

Analytically he scrutinized their movements, observing patterns, while another part of his brain calculated possibilities and probabilities. He really didn't care about these guys except for the fact that they'd messed up his operation.

He waited for the timed surveillance monitors to shift to the exterior view.

He sighed. The front tent was empty, no guards. They were likely stashed behind the larger ceramic urns that flanked the doorway. At the rear entrance, blood splattered the door and porch. The guards were nowhere to be seen, but to avoid suspicion they'd likely been dragged to the side of the garage. Based on that splatter pattern and the amount of blood, he guessed they were dead.

"What do you see?" she whispered.

Couldn't keep her down for long.

"Bad guys with guns."

He hoped that the ambassador was paranoid enough not to have cameras in the hidden room or this elevator, otherwise they were fucked.

There were no suspicious assault vehicles or jeeps in front of or behind the house. Only the expensive, valet parked cars in front. The driveway was clear to the garage in back. Nothing on the exterior indicated that the home had been overtaken by thugs.

Finally, the men were through the hallway. Ken hopped to his feet and pressed the button. He needed to get his date to the basement room, now while no one could hear them, and the invaders were nowhere near.

The lift whirred quietly to life. Ken held out his hand to help Barb up but kept his gaze squarely on the monitors. Damn he wished he had a weapon. Although one small handgun against assault rifles was like bringing a switchblade to a swordfight.

Barb curled her fingers around his and he yanked her to her feet.

The elevator very quietly made its way to the underground bunker. The doors slid open.

Ken tugged his companion out of the elevator.

Her gaze was wide, shell-shocked, but she wasn't screaming and she wasn't passed out from terror. So maybe next time he saw Jamie, he'd thank her instead of yell at her.

"Holy Batman's Lair," she said in awe.

Ken chuckled. She wasn't far off.

The square room was nothing like the upstairs design. Stark white walls were lined with gray cabinets. A long console along the wall to the right held an elaborate computer setup. Monitors embedded in the wall above the computers transmitted the same views that were displayed in the elevator. To the left of the elevator were two floor-to-ceiling cabinets.

To the right of the computer set up, another bank of low cabinets ran the length of the wall and treasures of varying periods were laid out in precise rows. Directly across from the elevator was a single chair and ottoman with a small end table holding a lamp, an ash tray, and a jade vase with several sprays of cherry blossom branches. On the wall above the chair hung a painting depicting the famous gardens at Changdeok Palace. The faint odor of Raison Red cigarette smoke and a hint of decay lingered in the air.

The ambassador's secret room.

25

Hopefully, they could get what Ken came for and get the hell out.

Too bad he didn't know exactly what he was looking for.

Before beginning his search, he popped open the engineering panel for the elevator and studied the configuration of the box. After a few seconds, he pulled out a crucial fuse. In case the intruders found the elevator he wanted time to figure out how to get his date the hell out.

"You disabled the elevator?"

He nodded sharply, then mentally moved on to his next task. He had to find the files he was looking for. But he hadn't planned on doing this with his date in tow.

"What is this place?" she whispered, like they were in a church.

"Super-secret bunker." His mouth quirked, thinking back to her earlier snarky comment. "So I guess you got your spy wish. You're in."

A snort of laughter escaped before she could subdue it, and the look of surprise on her face was priceless.

"Have a seat." He gestured to a leather-and-chrome chair at the sleek modern console. "Rest. You should be safe here."

Barb dropped into the desk chair with a relieved sigh. She pressed one hand over her heart and closed her eyes.

Ken started systematically searching the desk.

This was a golden opportunity. He'd been obsessed with getting access to the ambassador's private files since he'd finally narrowed down his suspects, and he wasn't about to let some asshole terrorists ruin his opportunity to search Choi's private records about what really happened during the Gwangju Uprising.

It had taken years of building trust and making human intelligence connections to get to the point where he could get into this secret room. An espionage counterpart, and sometimes co-conspirator, Carson Black had finally come through and gotten him the access code for this room. According to Black, the code changed every day. Only the ambassador and his secretary had access to the random generator. So this was a one-time deal. He couldn't afford to blow this opportunity. This was Ken's shot.

If the proof wasn't here, he'd have to start all over.

It was stupid to put all his focus in one place, but all his searching, his compiling of evidence, and his snooping had led to Ambassador Choi and the rumored speculation of a secret room.

So far nothing about this mission had gone as planned. His date was far too smart. His mind kept straying to more personal, physical things while he was in her presence. And now he had to deal with a group of armed thugs invading the party upstairs.

Although the more he thought about it, the more he realized that their party takeover was perfect. While the terrorists were holding hostages and taking up time, he could search this room. They were an excellent diversion. Instead of constantly watching the clock, he had a longer window to look for the evidence to prove that his father had not been a riot instigator, he had been pro-democracy and peaceful.

That was what Ken believed. That was what his mother had drilled into him all these years. His father was innocent. He was not, and had never been, a traitor.

And Ambassador Choi had been the one to initiate the deadly force and kill the peaceful protesters.

Of course Ken had investigated other officials who'd been in power during the fateful days of the Gwangju Uprising. All his other leads had been dead ends. There was only one link left unexplored.

Now Ken was in the position to find evidence that would support his beliefs.

If he were Choi, even in a top secret room, where would he keep that proof?

Ken dug through the file drawers.

It wasn't optimal that he had Barbie, the difficult date, watching him. But he could work around it.

She was suspiciously quiet. Hopefully she wasn't about to have a freak-out. Not that he would blame her. It certainly had been an eventful evening. And it wasn't over yet.

He meticulously flipped through the file cabinet.

"Why aren't you trying to figure out how to stop them?" she asked.

"One guy, against all those men?" Ken paused, gave her his best harmless smile. "I wouldn't stand a chance. I'm just a government lackey."

Not completely true but since he was right where he wanted to be, there was no way he was going to interfere in the drama above.

She eyed him as he continued to riffle through the desk. "What are you doing?"

"Looking for the key to the Bat Cave," he said flippantly.

"Seems to me you already had it." Her eyes rounded. "Who *are* you?"

"Look. With the power on and likely the Secret Service and FBI on the way—" at least he assumed the security team had been able to alert the authorities, "—everything will be okay." Just in case she was one step away from panic.

However, Barb didn't look panicked. She looked irritated, suspicious, gorgeous.

He said calmly, "We should be fine down here as long as the power stays on."

She opened her luscious mouth to dash off some snippy response—if her previous reactions to today's events ran true to form.

And the lights went out.

CHAPTER 4

The room plunged into darkness.

Great, what the hell else could go wrong? This was the worst date ever.

Though I would never admit it, it certainly hadn't been boring.

"*Shi-bal.*" Ken stopped his scrabbling through the filing cabinets. The hum of the lights and computers was gone. The room was deadly silent. No sound from above penetrated this hidden lair.

It was pitch black.

I leaned back in the ergonomic chair. I had no problem with the dark but the impenetrable black was disconcerting. Ken curled his fingers around my hand, his touch sure, solid. "You okay?"

The lack of sight heightened all my other senses. His breath hitched, just a small hiccup of sound. But he didn't seem the flappable type so I could only deduce that it was my touch, rather than the lack of sight. His spicy scent filled my head and I was overwhelmed by the dizzying rush of blood to my girl parts.

His fingers were callused and slightly rough as he stroked my hand as if to reassure me. The touch was a direct zap to my clit. I wanted his hands everywhere.

The want was so visceral, my vocal chords tightened. "Fine." My voice was husky.

But nothing was going to happen. Because my date had another agenda. He hadn't been looking for a way to communicate with the outside, he'd been searching this room. When I put that together with the fact that he'd had access to this secret room, either he worked for the ambassador, or he was invading the private, classified files of a diplomatic figure.

"Shouldn't be long now." He squeezed my palm, completely misunderstanding the rasp in my voice. With a sudden buzz, track lights illuminated along the floor, and the computers hummed back to life, starting the reboot process. The glow spread an eerie green light over his stark, masculine and yet, beautiful features.

He smiled softly. Oddly the gesture was sweet. And he didn't strike me as a sweet person. "Better?"

"I don't mind the dark." Of course my brain went straight to the other things we could be doing in the dark. Naked. Sweaty. Slick slide of skin against skin things.

"I do some of my best work in the dark." His voice was bland but there was a distinctly naughty flirtatiousness to his words.

I leaned toward that seductive smirk, wanting him to show me. The heat from his body washed over me, his breath soft against my mouth as we were drawn toward each other despite our obvious differences. He hovered above me, my pulse thundered in my ears, and my heart thudded in my chest, as all my senses arrowed onto his mouth like a heat-seeking missile locked on to a target.

Shit, I wanted him to kiss me again. If the fire in his eyes was any indication, we were on the same wavelength. He wanted it too.

Until the security monitors flickered back to life.

And the drama above us pushed out all thoughts of sexy times.

The terrorists had lined up all the party guests along the wall like they were awaiting a firing squad. And I hoped that even though my damn brain went there, that that wasn't what they were planning. To kill them all.

They were frisking the men one by one.

They shouted at the guests. Their mouths angry slashes in the hole of the masks, it was impossible to tell their ethnicity, but I thought by the shape of their heads and their compact muscular bodies that they were mostly of Asian descent. "Is there any way to get sound?" I whispered.

Ken studied the computer panels in front of him for a scant second. Then he pressed a series of buttons and suddenly we could hear. Unfortunately, what we heard wasn't very reassuring. I was sorry I'd asked.

The terrorists were shouting, demanding Ambassador Choi show himself. They shoved their masked faces into the personal space of the hostages, their body language intimidating and threatening.

They alternated yelling in English and French, waving their assault weapons menacingly. One of the gunmen lifted his weapon and took aim at the celadon ceramic Buddha displayed on a pedestal in the corner. With one true shot, the stone shattered, spraying shrapnel. The terrified hostages squealed and ducked their heads. One of the pieces hit the shooter near his exposed eye. Blood trickled over his mask, although he seemed impervious to the damage he'd done to his face.

He also didn't seem to care that he might be dripping DNA on the floor, which was a huge red flag for me.

Ken turned down the volume but their shouts were still loud in the dungeon-like basement.

"Where is the ambassador?" the leader screamed at the hostages.

"They don't know that he isn't here yet?" I asked.

There was something off with the way they were acting but for the life of me I had no idea what. My blood pulsed in the stifling thick air, this time from fear rather than desire. I preferred to be turned on, not terrified.

The emergency lights were on but there was little in the way of ventilation and the room was already becoming warm.

Ken must have thought the same because while I was watching the monitors, he'd removed his uniform jacket and was now in the process of unbuttoning his white dress shirt.

Ken assessed the terrorists on the monitor. "Perhaps."

"They aren't very efficient then, are they?" My voice was breathy, not my usual matter-of-fact tone. As a woman in the sciences I had to work extra hard to be taken seriously, which meant that I mostly hid my femininity behind a gruff exterior and no-nonsense attitude. But he was disrupting my normal way of dealing with people, and I was off balance.

He paused in the act of taking off his shirt, baring one perfect, beautifully-muscled shoulder and revealing the white wifebeater beneath.

My breath stopped in my throat. Because while I'd been mostly sarcastic about his muscles, or lack of muscles, I'd been wrong.

He was absolutely ripped. His abs rippled beneath the tight white tank. And suddenly the heat in the room wasn't just from the computer equipment. My body flushed with a vicious burst of ill-timed lust.

I must have made some small sound. A quick inhale, a startled "oh." Because Ken shifted his gaze from the monitors to me, and his stare pierced me with a curious intensity. As if he could see inside to my lonely core and strip me of all my defenses, the look penetrated and laid me bare more intimately than sex. My entire body primed.

His black gaze smoldered, transmitting a ripe sexual hunger.

In a heartbeat, he pressed me against the console, his arms bracketing my body, and heat shimmered between us like a living breathing force. His mouth was a bare centimeter from mine. Sexual energy buzzed, power and current arcing in a dangerous burst, hurling around us in a frenzied storm.

The tension in the room ratcheted to an excruciating degree. "What are we going to do?" I didn't know if I was asking about the terrorists or the kiss waiting to happen. I just knew that I needed him to give me an answer.

His gaze dropped to my lips and dammit, I wanted him to kiss me. I wasn't even sure I liked him but holy hell did I want him.

His body appeared loose, supple even, but his eyes burned with a fierce intensity that told me he was as hyper-focused on me as I was on him. The thought was heady, exhilarating, intoxicating. He wanted me too.

Kiss me.

He leaned closer until anticipation burned in my blood. I wanted his mouth on mine so fucking badly. Even though we were in the middle of a frightening situation, we were safe here in this basement bunker for a few moments. I wanted him to kiss me. I *needed* him to kiss me.

His breath was warm against the sensitive curve of my neck. Goosebumps peppered my skin as I waited for him to press his mouth to mine. His erection swelled until he brushed the curve of my belly.

I waited for him. To take. To ravage. To…dominate.

I wanted it all.

His nose brushed my ear, the only place our bodies touched, and the contact sent a vicious chill over my spine as he paused, letting expectation heighten. Then he whispered, "We're going to wait to be rescued."

As if he'd popped a balloon, all that anticipation pffftted out of me in a blast of air.

I tried to wrap some spectrum of professionalism around me like a shield. I didn't want my disappointment to come through so I made my voice brusque. "Right." I couldn't step back from him, because he still pinned me to the console with the cage of his body.

The urge to punch him, to get him to back off was strong. Very strong.

His face was a bland mask as if he weren't affected by the pheromones swirling between us. But as much as he might try to misdirect my attention, his cock was still a thick pole in his pants, straining toward me.

If I arched at all, his body would caress mine again. So he could pretend all he wanted, but his body didn't lie.

Finally, Ken stepped away from me. As if he'd flipped off that power beam, his face settled into a concentrated frown and he went back to digging through the files in the drawer.

I watched him comb carefully through the contents. I trusted my instincts implicitly. He wasn't looking for communication devices or a way out of here. He was looking for something else.

My gaze kept drifting to the monitors and the violence that seemed almost like a movie. Like it had been staged for maximum effect.

I knew he wouldn't tell me what he was looking for. So I proceeded to nag him. To direct his attention where I wanted it. On figuring out how to help those people.

"We can't just…stay down here and hide."

"Why ever not, *chagiya*?" He didn't even look up from his search.

"What does that mean?"

He distracted me with the truth. "Roughly translated, *darling.*"

"I'm not your darling." My temper took quite a bit to rile but he was needling me quite spectacularly. "Those people up there need our help," I insisted.

"The safest thing we can do is let the drama play out."

Safe. He wasn't safe. That vapid, vain man who'd escorted me into the party might be discounted. But I'd seen beneath that façade to the warrior. I racked my brain for something we could do. "You're the super-secret spy. Figure something out."

"Super-secret spies work in the shadows." Ken ignored me and continued riffling through the files.

Now he was making fun of me. I grabbed his arm. His skin was supple, smooth, hot beneath my palm. The contact sizzled up my arm and zapped my heart. "We have to do something!"

"We really don't."

"They're going to kill those people."

"Likely not." He continued to flip through the files.

"We can't just stand idly by and hope those people don't get massacred." Reaction from earlier was setting in. I ruthlessly subdued the tremble in my limbs. If I started to fall apart, he'd never do what I wanted. "Otherwise, we're no better than the terrorists hurting them."

He paused, everything about him went so still that I couldn't even see him breathe. I'd struck a nerve. A deep one apparently. But I didn't know if that would be enough to get him to focus on something bigger than whatever he was doing.

His head dropped. His eyes closed. He seemed to be saying a prayer.

What he wasn't doing was coming up with a plan or bursting into action to help the hostages above.

"I'm going to kill Jamie," I muttered. This was stupid. I was a freaking smart, accomplished woman. "I don't need some pretty boy to help these people."

Once again I'd been put in a situation where I could make a difference. With a little help. The lure of clandestine operations fizzed in my blood like an illicit drug.

I'd helped Jamie and Lucas. Together they had saved the day and fallen in love. Theirs was an epic love story.

Was it so wrong to want one of my own?

No, it wasn't. But the only way I was going to get an epic love story was if I got out of here and found a guy on my own.

Because Ken Park sure as hell wasn't the one.

Ken snorted. "Did you just call me a pretty boy?"

He crowded me up against the console again. My traitorous body responded to his even though my brain was telling me that he could give a fuck about the people above us. Or me. His breath feathered against my neck, and heat from his body surrounded me like a glove. Damn him.

We were in the same position as a moment ago when I'd waited for him to kiss me.

Why had I waited? Normally I take what I want. I own my sexuality. I wasn't some shy delicate flower who needed a man to show her the way. I'd forged my own path in my life. In my career. That naturally bled over into my dating life. But for some reason, I had waited for him to make the move. Dammit. Not doing that again.

I put my hands on his chest to shove him away.

His pecs flexed.

My mouth dried as I forgot what we were talking about. Oh, yeah. Pretty boys. I got my mouth in line with my brain. "Yeah."

"I'm not a boy." He hovered over me, his presence dominating but I refused to be cowed.

He definitely wasn't.

And I'd definitely noticed.

"You want to help those people? Do a count of how many people, hostages, are in the room. Do a count of the terrorists. Write down any details that strike you. Anything that seems out of the ordinary. How many weapons are they each carrying? Guns, knives, throwing stars. How are they communicating? What do they want?"

His voice had shifted from seductive to commanding. The change was abrupt, disconcerting. But it was as if the veneer had been peeled away and I could see him clearly now. Nothing distorted him. I saw the warrior I'd sensed earlier. The one deserving of all those medals on his chest.

He tossed a notebook at me.

"What are we going to do with the information?"

"Plan," he clipped out. "We can't just go off half-cocked."

My gaze slipped to his crotch.

Ken smirked. "Not now, darling," he purred, trying to distract me, but this time it wasn't going to work.

"They know the ambassador isn't here." I gestured to the monitor that showed the main reception room.

The ambassador's teenaged son lay on the floor, clearly injured, but he wasn't dead. That was good. But he'd had the shit beat out of him.

"How do you know?"

"They're fucking with the hostage's heads." I pointed to the terrorist who was the leader. "He said they'd let everyone go if they would just give up the ambassador but if you look—" I followed his pacing movements with my finger, noting that he didn't stop and look anyone in the eye, "—he has no intention of releasing anyone. He's lying."

Which did not give me warm fuzzies. Because I had no idea if his body language meant he wasn't going to let them go *right now*, or if his body language meant he wasn't going to let them go *ever*.

So there was another game going on beneath the surface.

"How can you tell?" Ken watched the leader's movements.

"He isn't even angry. He's putting on a show."

He cocked his head, shifted his attention to me. "You study

body language?"

"I'm a scientist at heart." I studied the man's actions. Studied the way he strutted around the room, his movements fluid and rolling. "I study everything."

The leader's yelling, posturing was all for show. The question was for who?

The hostages? Someone else? They had to want something more than just the ambassador. It was almost as if…they were waiting. But what were they waiting for?

"Good point." He couldn't be more condescending if he'd patted me on the damn head. I cocked my hip, propped my fist, and tilted my head. Really?

"We need more intel," Ken said abruptly. "We need details before we plan a rescue. We need a threat assessment."

"What are you going to be doing?"

"Dictating."

He'd lost all the sexy times from his demeanor. He was still going through the files in the drawers. But he seemed to be splitting his attention between whatever he actually came here to do and me.

Another thought occurred to me. "Are you with them?"

Maybe that was why he didn't care what was happening upstairs. The entire invasion was to mask what he was doing down here in this secret room.

He glanced at me, then went back to what he was doing.

No fucking way was he dismissing me. Even as I had that thought, I had a moment of WTF was I thinking?

"If I am, baiting me is not in your best interests."

The charming sycophant was completely obliterated by a hard, intense warrior. Instead of being afraid…shit, all my girl parts stood up and took notice.

If I thought he was attractive when he was a fawning metrosexual, this new harder side of him was magnetic and enthralling.

CHAPTER 5

J esus, she practically sizzled with sexual energy.

Ken needed to crack down and focus on his mission.

He couldn't believe he'd forgotten where they were and what was at stake. He'd almost plunged into what was sure to be another mind-blowing kiss. If the violence on the monitor hadn't caught his peripheral vision he would have been all over her.

He didn't get distracted by women. Ever.

But for a brief moment, all he could think about was her. Him. And hot, sweaty spectacular sex.

So he'd pulled back, pissed her off.

However, he needed Barb as an asset. She wasn't going to let this go. And while he might have some sympathy for the people upstairs, he'd come here with an agenda, one he'd spent most of his life pursuing.

So, yeah, her wants didn't even really register on his personal Richter scale.

But if he didn't appease her, she'd just keep at him.

"You make notes, talk to me." Ken continued to look through

the filing cabinet, searching for any reference to the Gwangju Uprising.

He couldn't afford to blow this opportunity. He couldn't guarantee he could get back in this room ever again. The security in the residence would be ramped up after this incident.

Yes, that was harsh, cold, and he didn't give a fuck. He'd been searching since he was a child to find the truth about his father's involvement in the uprising.

"How many terrorists?"

"Five."

"That we can see," Ken said. "Assume they're like rodents. What you see is only part of the infestation."

He slammed the first drawer shut. Dammit, this was going to take forever. A bead of sweat rolled down his temple.

Go-saeng Ggeut-eh naki eun-da. He silently repeated the mantra his mother had drilled into him for his entire life: *"At the end of hardship comes happiness."*

The Gwangju Uprising occurred in 1980. Back before digital files were really a thing. And Ambassador Choi was old school. He'd have a paper copy of evidence that would prove what really happened.

Ken was damn sure that Choi would have documentation and evidence that exonerated him or implicated others. The man was notorious for protecting his own ass.

He opened the next drawer. The files were labeled by political figures, specific treaties, agreements between The Republic of Korea and various allies.

He flipped through more files until he got to the end. They seemed to be standard files that a diplomat might have in a secure safe location. They were tagged by date and event. He found the drawer marked with the time frame he needed to review.

His date had stopped scribbling on the paper he'd given her.

Better keep her occupied so she didn't focus on what he was doing.

"How are they communicating?"

"They're all in the main room."

"Doubtful," Ken said. "They need lookouts for each entrance/exit. Possibly more than one. Watch the screens."

She leaned over the desk counter and peered at the monitors.

The rounded globes of her ass pulled his attention from the file folders as she pushed up on tiptoe.

Not the time to get distracted by a gorgeous ass. The back of her dress fell in an open drape exposing the lean line of her spine, and revealing a barely there lace bra. A fine layer of sweat sheened her chocolate skin, gleaming in the close, heated air, and a perfume of sweet flowers and spicy citrus scented the small room. The delicious smell made his mouth water, and he was tempted to press close and lick her skin. Totally inappropriate.

"They have earpieces in."

"So presumably they have someone coordinating the operation who can hear what they're saying."

Ken dragged his attention away from the lickability of her skin and refocused on the contents of the drawer.

He spot-checked inside the file folders, searching for something, anything relating to the uprising. Shit. The answers *had* to be in this room.

"Several of the guys have backpacks," Barb said. "What do you think is in them?"

Nothing good. "Lunch?"

"Quit being a smartass."

"Extra ammunition. Communication devices."

"They aren't looking for anything."

Ken ran his gaze over the wall opposite the computer setup. The single chair and book told their own story. A jade vase was filled with three stalks of bare cherry tree branches. The petals littered the small tabletop. Something about the framed photograph of the palace garden drew his attention. He stalked closer, examining the picture. He lifted the frame off the wall and sure enough, there was a Brown safe.

He hadn't had this information. He jumped up on the chair to peer at the dimensions and get an idea of how difficult it would be to crack.

"What are you doing?" She sounded crabby.

"Exploring." Ken wasn't about to spill his secrets.

"Dammit. You are a spy," she said glumly.

He continued examining the safe trying to figure out what it would take to get it open. He ran his fingers along the edges of the matte metal. Pressed a button and a panel swung open.

Yes!

He'd need a password. The Franklin Group used the GSA ComSec approved Brown Safes for their computer equipment and other sensitive documents. But this safe looked nothing like the one they had in their office.

Clearly the safe was custom. Because instead of a keypad, the safe had an infrared biometric scanner large enough for an entire hand. Shit. He'd need a palm print, which he definitely didn't have. He didn't even want to chance touching the reader in case the safe had a warning system in place.

No sense setting off alarms elsewhere and alerting the terrorists to their presence. *"Jen-jang."* The safe was a dead end.

"What's that mean?"

"It means I can't get in."

But the more he thought about it, the more he thought that Choi wouldn't have the information stored in one place. Like a squirrel ferreting away nuts, he would have multiple hiding places. If anything the safe was probably a diversion.

He wondered about the group of treasures on the countertop. Could the information be stored in one of them?

He hopped down and stalked to the long counter.

"What are those?"

Ken studied the varying statues and vases. Some looked to be quite old. "Choi's brother is a known dealer of antiquities."

"Okay."

But something about the pieces in this room bothered him. If he wasn't mistaken, the celadon Buddha looked damn similar to the one upstairs.

"Aren't there rules about removing cultural treasures from their home countries?"

"Yeah. But the ambassador's residence is technically Korean soil."

"So in this house they aren't considered removed." Barb's eyebrows rose.

There had been murmurings about Choi's brother, about smuggling or dealing in stolen antiquities, but the authorities had never been able to find any evidence on him. And it wasn't illegal for Choi to benefit from his brother's legitimate business. But what if....

"That kinda looks like the one they shot upstairs." Barb peered at the religious statue.

What if the one upstairs was a copy? Choi wouldn't be the first to display fakes in order to safeguard them from being stolen, but something seemed off about that too. Under each statue, or vase, was a provenance certificate. Ken pulled one out, distracted against his will by the inconsistency.

Barb asked, "What are you thinking?"

"Maybe the ambassador is participating in a little illegal art and antiquities dealing." Could that be what the men upstairs wanted? These artifacts? This was a robbery?

"So you can expose him once we're out of here?" Barb replied. "Is that what you were looking to find?"

He remained silent.

"What aren't you telling me?"

There was an entire history book full of intelligence he wasn't sharing with her. "Nothing."

43

"Bullshit."

The swear word seemed almost obscene coming out of her mouth.

He had to give her something. "I don't like being trapped down here and unable to fight." Which was in some ways true, but not the whole truth. He didn't like being trapped down here.

He definitely hated the fact that she was trapped.

She rolled her eyes. "Damn, Jamie."

Ken paused. He realized she'd mentioned Jamie earlier. She knew Jamie's real name? That was unusual. "How do you know Jamie again?"

"Mutual friend."

"Jamie doesn't have friends." He should know. He didn't either.

"Right?" Barb stepped back from the counter and tilted her head, watching the violent action happening above their heads on the small black-and-white screen. "What the hell do they want?"

"What do most terrorists want?" he asked patiently as he pawed through another set of files. He'd gone back to his first search parameter, because the safe was a dead end unless he could find a spare hand print of the ambassador's lying around, and while the treasures were a mystery, he needed to stick to his original mission.

He needed to find the intelligence that would clear his father's name.

"To strike terror," she whispered. "But what's their exit strategy?"

Ken shoved another drawer closed. Nothing. Dammit. He needed to get his shit together and figure out where the hell Ambassador Choi would have hidden the file.

Something about her words reverberated in his head.

"Exit strategy, exit strategy." A huge smile burst from him. "Yes!"

He grabbed her by the hips and yanked her toward him.
Barb slammed against his chest and her arms went around his
back involuntarily.

He cupped her face in his palms and slanted his mouth over
hers in a celebratory kiss.

She'd cracked the ambassador's code without even trying.

He meant for this to be a quick caress. But Ken got lost in
the pleasure of her mouth. She'd surrendered with little protest,
and began kissing him back. She skimmed her hands over his
bare shoulders, trailing goosebumps in her wake. Her breasts
pillowed against his pecs and her hips cradled his erection.
Pleasure bombarded him as they dueled with erotic abandon.
The longing to dive in, to get lost in her body, was strong. But
they didn't have time for that right now. Ken disengaged
their lips.

"You're a genius." His voice was far huskier than he'd like
even as he gave her a genuine smile.

"You have a dimple," she blurted out. She traced her finger
around his mouth, over the slight indent that rarely made an
appearance. Her light touch zapped through him in a line
straight to his dick.

"I need to stay focused." As if she were tempting him. When
in reality he'd put temptation in his own path.

They broke apart awkwardly.

Ken regretted the loss of her touch as she pretended to study
the monitors on the wall. But she'd given him a new avenue to
pursue. Choi wouldn't have this information in a file cabinet.
He'd have a Go Bag somewhere in this room.

Choi would want the information on his person, or as close as
he could get in case of the need for an unexpected exodus. Go
Bag meant he needed to be looking for a closet or a deep drawer.
Someplace big enough to store the Ambassador's prized
possessions.

Ken skimmed his gaze over the layout of the room, searching

for anything odd in the dimensions that might indicate a secret hollow or drawer.

He opened the floor-to-ceiling doors on the wall to the left of the elevator.

The shallow pantry held canned goods, a twenty-pound bag of rice, a small hot plate, and easily fifty gallons of water. One shelf had two small cooking pots, plates, glasses, and utensils. The last held blankets, pillows, and battery-operated camping lanterns. The ambassador had enough food and supplies to last a thirty-day siege.

"Looks like we're covered."

The next set of doors revealed a small water closet with a toilet and sink.

But as Ken studied the bathroom he realized that the storage closet didn't have the same measurements as the bathroom.

Ken yanked open the pantry doors and studied the interior. He knelt down and eyed the dimensions. There was confirmation. The shelves were too shallow. There was missing square footage. It was hard to see in the dim light. Choi would want fast access so the lever needed to be on a shelf that didn't have too much stuff in front of it.

He'd bet the ambassador's Go Bag was stored behind these shelves.

Ken ran his fingers along the back of the cabinet, looking for a seam or anything to indicate that there was a way in to the hidden compartment.

"What are you doing?" Barb's voice was muffled since Ken had most of his head buried underneath the shelf that held the towels.

"Grab one of those lanterns and turn it on," he directed her. Right now he was going mostly on feel. He traced his fingertips along the wall, carefully testing, looking for the lever or the trigger to access what he was sure was the entrance to a hidden compartment.

Within seconds she was back. "Got one." The lantern buzzed to life.

"Point the light at the back of the cabinet."

The space remained dark.

"Do I get to find out what you're doing?"

No one ever knew what he was doing. "Sure."

"You are such a liar," she muttered. The light clicked on and he could see more of the back panel. And there in the corner, he found the seam. But where was the lever that would open the panel?

Found it. Ken's heart boomed and his breath was short. He pressed on the edge and the camouflaged door slid sideways into a pocket and revealed a secret storage space. The compartment could hold two, maybe three, people but what caught his eye was the large duffel on the floor. The duffel bag, coated with dust, was the sole item in the small space.

"What did you find?" Barb's breath blew hot on his neck.

Everything. "Probably nothing."

Ken's hand trembled as he reached inside the concealed compartment. He stopped, inhaled, held his breath.

His heartbeat echoed in his ears.

Ken pulled it out carefully.

"What do you think is inside?"

"Aren't you supposed to be watching the monitors?" Ken didn't want her intruding on this very private moment.

She huffed out an irritated breath. "Fine."

Ken waited until she was on the other side of the room before he delicately unzipped the duffel. The weight of this moment pressed in on him. He worked his whole life to find the evidence to exonerate his father, the proof that the government had willfully opened fire on the peaceful protesters. To finally expose Jung-ho Choi for the murderer Ken knew him to be.

Everything in his life had been building toward this moment. Exposing the people responsible for the deaths of hundreds had been his purpose in life since he was old enough to talk. His mother had drilled the goal of vengeance into him since he'd been in the crib. And if he was correct, the instrument to wield that vengeance was at hand.

He peered inside the bag.

He needed to document everything. His watch also doubled as a camera and storage device. Surreptitiously he began to snap pictures of the contents as he removed them from the Go Bag.

Forged French passports—for the ambassador, his wife, and his son—under assumed names.

Two pre-paid burner cells.

Ken pressed a button and powered up a cell phone. He tossed it to Barb. "See if you can get a signal."

Her face lit up. "A phone!"

He continued to paw through the bag. Small pistol. Ammunition. Titanium throwing stars. A wicked-looking Karambit knife.

He stowed the blade of the curved steel knife into its retracted position and then tucked the deadly weapon into his pants pocket. Then he continued to catalog the contents of the bag.

Several cartons of Raison Red cigarettes. Ken raised a brow. Someone had a serious nicotine addiction.

Three sets of nondescript clothing and plain canvas shoes.

Stacks of money. Korean won. Euros. US dollars. Ken flipped through the banded money then tossed it back in the bag. Money didn't interest him.

A small pouch of utility tools, screwdriver, wrench, ball-peen hammer. He considered the pouch, then put that in his other pocket.

Deep in the bottom of the bag was a manila envelope thick with papers.

Her dejected sigh broke through his concentration. "No bars."

Ken pressed the metal tabs together and opened the clasp on the old-fashioned manila envelope.

"They're taking the ambassador's wife out of the room now."

"Where are they taking her?" Ken asked distractedly. One side of his brain was still functioning normally while the other was frozen.

Sweat rolled down the side of his face as he shook the papers from the envelope. He flipped through the pages, ignoring the labels on top of the files. He could come back to the documents that might also have political implications later. The documents appeared to be in chronological order.

With his watch, he snapped pictures of each page, only skimming the contents. Until he got to the page he'd been looking for. The page that defined his entire life.

Right there in black and white was the confirmation Ken had been searching for. The memo outlined the new government's position on the protestors and the decision to use force against them. The pro-democracy peaceful protest needed to be crushed. The new government couldn't afford to appear weak in any form. So the new leader had ordered the army to fire on the protesters and leak to the media that they were rabble-rousing dissidents. It was written and signed by the new leader, but Choi had been the executor. He had been tasked with killing the protestors.

Ken couldn't move. It was the conclusive proof he'd been searching for. The reason his mother had fled the country. The reason he had never known his father.

He should be elated. Literally every decision in his life had been influenced by the events of May 18. Since he was a child, he'd been searching for proof that his father was an innocent. And now that he held that proof in his hands, he just felt…numb.

What do I do next?

CHAPTER 6

K en's hand shook. He willed his limbs stable as he shot a picture of the document.

He had to wonder if Carson Black had known what he would find.

Carson had been the one to get him the code to the elevator. He'd been the one who'd facilitated his access to this party.

The old spy was wily. Always plotting and moving the pieces two or three steps ahead of his opponents. That was why he was the director of Field Ops for the super-secret branch of the NSA. Most people, even in the espionage community, didn't know that the Field Ops division even existed.

Carson Black ran it all with a dedication to secrecy that almost surpassed Ken's own. And fuck him, he had to wonder... what had prompted Carson to give him this intelligence for today?

Ken had been double-crossed before. Lived to tell no one. He'd basically been double-crossing Korean intelligence since he was eighteen. He'd played both sides. Anything to find out the truth.

What had Carson known before he sent Ken here?

Ken couldn't even ask Carson. To ask was to admit that he'd found something.

Of course, everyone would know what he'd found. He was planning to expose Choi, reveal to the world that the ambassador had been responsible for one of the largest massacres in Korean history, that Choi had killed his own people, not by accident but in cold blood.

He damn well hoped that Carson didn't have his own agenda. That worry felt like a particularly sharp betrayal knife in his gut.

"What's wrong?" she whispered, the words loud in the fraught silence.

Now he wondered if Barb's presence was also a betrayal. She was more intelligent than the average woman. She hadn't freaked out at the shooting, she hadn't freaked out at the secret room, she'd rolled with the rapidly changing circumstances like a pro.

In one violent burst, Ken held her against the wall next to the elevator, his grip tight and hard over her hyoid bone. "Did Carson place you?"

Barb had gone completely still. No struggling. No attempt to get free. But the look in her deep brown eyes told him that she understood the precariousness of her position.

Because she wasn't resisting, he loosened his grip. After all there was nowhere for her to go. They were stuck down here while there were terrorists above.

Was that why she was so intent on his movements and his actions? Was that why she hadn't completely freaked out about the terrorists above their heads? Because Carson Black had set him up and given him a shadow so that when he discovered the truth about what happened on May 18, 1980, someone would be watching?

If so, what was she supposed to do once he found the proof? What was her mission objective? To make sure he revealed the truth? Or to stop him from letting the world know what had really happened?

"Why don't you tell me, Barbie?" he snarled, unwilling to believe she was innocent. No one in this world was innocent anymore.

"Yeah, don't call me Barbie." She knocked his hand away from her throat. But it wasn't a practiced martial arts move. It was clumsy, awkward. And wouldn't have worked unless he let it. "I don't know what your problem is, but I've about had it." She began to pace. "I've had a crappy week."

Ken raised his eyebrows.

"I've realigned my priorities, figured out I want a baby, which frankly is insane. But my damn biological clock is spinning like an electric meter out of control, and I don't have a prospective baby daddy. Then Jamie freaking Hunt, who I thought was becoming my friend, sets me up with, with *you*…and all the sudden I'm in the middle of some hostage situation that you don't even seem to care about. So forgive me if I don't jump to answer your bidding. As far as I'm concerned you are on Team Asshole and not on Team Barb."

Ken snorted. "Team Asshole?"

"*That's* what you focus on?" Barb threw up her hands. "Not all the other shit, but the fact that I think you're an asshole."

He held in a laugh. A big one.

Amusement gurgled in his belly, unexpected and surprising. He didn't laugh. Things didn't amuse him. Life was one big deadly situation that required severe intensity and focused attention at all times. There was no room for laughter.

She could be playing him. He gauged the probability that she had a different agenda. The possibility was more than fifty percent. But he couldn't remember the last time he laughed and meant it.

She still hadn't answered his question. A fact that had not escaped his notice. She hadn't even blinked at Carson's name.

If she were trained, she'd know to avoid admitting anything. Deflect and distract without denying. She'd managed to do both with seemingly little effort. And yet he didn't like her for an agent, and he'd never been wrong before.

He had an almost preternatural ability to detect subterfuge.

He didn't get that vibe from Barb at all. He also could be thinking with his dick. Again not something he typically did, but nothing about today, about their *date*, was typical.

"Did he?"

Barb's forehead crinkled as if she was trying to work out his true question. "Of course not. I don't even know who that is." But her manner had changed, not placating, more confused.

"Jamie's boss."

"Why would Jamie's boss set me up on a blind date?"

The other things she said registered.

"You want a baby?" Ken shuddered.

"Yeah." All her energy seemed to deflate. "I'm thirty-four. I've done a lot. I'm ready."

"What about the daddy?" He couldn't help but be curious. He really had more important things to be worrying about, but her confession had seemed to be wrung from a hidden place deep inside.

"Yeah, well, that does seem to be the problem." Barb wiped the sweat from her brow. "Don't take this the wrong way because I'm in no way suggesting you for the position, but don't you want kids?"

He blinked. Thought. Searched his brain. "I've never really thought about it."

"Never?" She brushed at some strands of hair that had fallen into his eyes. "No little Park to carry on your family name."

The tender gesture took him aback. "No. It's hard to think about the future when you are chained to the past."

And fuck him, that was how he thought about his life lately. He was too chained to a mission, to his family's honor, to think about a future beyond finding the people responsible for his father's death.

"Chained to the past?" Compassion flooded her gaze. Her whole face softened, sweetened. "What has you shackled to the past?"

"It's not important." A lie, of course. It was the only thing that was important. To avenge his father. Family honor. The basis for everything he'd undertaken in his life.

Noise from the monitor drew both their attention. The violence was escalating.

One of the terrorists shoved the ambassador's wife.

They were in the study. Ken could see the stack of invitations on the desk, which meant that the micro-thin listening patch was transmitting to Carson. Hopefully some nameless, faceless employee at the NSA was picking up that there was a problem, a big one, at this embassy party and had alerted the authorities.

"May 18!" the terrorist screamed in Soo-jin Choi's face. The leader clutched her by her perfectly coiffed hair and shook her like a rag doll. "Where does he keep his shame?"

Ken jolted.

These mercenaries wanted information about the Gwangju Uprising? What were the odds that they would storm the ambassador's residence on the same day and party as he did, covertly looking for the same information he was? Not good.

Something more was at play here.

Barb intruded on his thoughts. "What is May 18?"

"May 18 is the date of the Gwangju Uprising."

"What happened?"

"In 1980, after a series of incidents, the new government imposed martial law. A group of students and university employees instigated a peaceful demonstration to support democracy and protest the martial law. The conflict escalated and the army opened fire on the protesters and hundreds of people died." May 18, the day the path of his life changed forever.

"That's terrible." She was watching the monitor intently. "But it was a long time ago, why would they bring it up now?"

"There have always been questions about what really happened that day and in the days afterward. Documents were destroyed so that the people would never know if the government's intent was to inflict violence on the students and other protesters."

"So that's what they want." Barb's gaze slid to the files he'd found.

He needed to distract her quickly. He grabbed the weapon from the Go Bag and handed it to her. "You know how to shoot?"

She shuddered. "A gun?"

"No. A bow and arrow," he snarked.

"No."

Shit. Well that was not encouraging. "Point. Aim for a center mass. Something big. This weapon doesn't have a safety. Just pull the trigger."

She accepted the weapon gingerly. "Why are you telling me this?"

Ken needed to get the information he'd just photographed somewhere safe. The device in his watch saved the pictures and then would transmit the data to a secure online cloud once he got in range of a functioning wireless connection.

It seemed illogical that the ambassador wouldn't have a way to communicate with the outside world in this hidden office. However, he was old school. Ken lifted up the landline. No dial tone.

The mercenaries had clearly cut the lines. No one had cell phones. Security had confiscated everyone's phone before they'd been allowed entrance into the party. Besides which, they had no signal down here.

"If we can't find a way to communicate with the outside…" Ken paused. Because it had been long enough that if the authorities had been alerted, there would be some movement outside the residence. Yet the surroundings were eerily silent.

"We need to find a way to get a message to someone that the party has been compromised and the attendees are hostages," she finished with dejection. "I understand that."

Ken nodded.

"What made you change your mind?" she asked.

He couldn't tell her the truth. "You did."

"Really," she replied flatly. She eyed the bag as if she knew he was lying through his perfectly straightened teeth.

"Unless we can find a way to communicate from this office, I need to go."

Before he ventured upstairs, they needed to look through everything in the office.

"We might luck out and find an internet box down here."

But a quick search of the drawers and the pantry confirmed they were empty of any kind of electronic equipment to connect to the outside world. He studied the movements of the terrorists. "I need to get upstairs and get the internet Wi-Fi back online."

Ken had a feeling that the terrorists had only disabled the house's internet capability rather than completely taken it out. After all, they would need a way to transmit their demands, assuming they had them, to the appropriate authorities. One could make the assumption that they were waiting for the ambassador to get here. Even though there were other high-value targets in attendance.

Ransom didn't seem to be their motive since they hadn't really targeted anyone but the ambassador's family.

"Are you sure the internet box is up there?" Barb asked dubiously.

"Yes. You stay here. Stay safe." *Stay out of my way, while I get the internet reconnected and get my intelligence uploaded.*

Depending on the terrorists' coverage of the house, he'd just head out and let Barb get rescued along with everyone else. He could escape, release the information, and let Carson and Jamie know where their girlfriend was stashed.

"You're going to stay here and watch. And listen," Ken commanded her.

Barb's body stiffened. A slight sheen of sweat glistened at her hairline. She had to be sweltering in that dress.

Her black lashes curved down, hiding her eyes.

He noted the action on the screen. The terrorist was still interrogating the ambassador's wife. She dangled from his fist as he whipped his pistol across her face. She'd stopped screaming and hung defeated, whimpering.

"Let me give you the code to get into the garage." And yeah, he was fucking giving away state secrets right now but damn, she needed a way out if something happened to him before he could get this information to his storage base and connect with the authorities. There might be a vehicle there she could use.

"Why would I need the garage code?" Barb asked. "You're the super-secret spy guy. You'll get us, me, out of here."

Ken just looked at her steadily. "This is the code."

"Nothing is going to happen to you." Barb's face took on a mutinous cast.

Her steadfast belief in him gave him a moment of guilt for leaving her alone.

He absorbed the disappointment he felt. He'd lost the opportunity to explore her body. And once he left her here he doubted she'd want a do-over of their date. Not to mention she wanted kids.

He had never even considered children. His life, his family had been characterized by a legacy of violence and disillusionment. Not happening.

And, he knew better than most, that battle was unpredictable.

If he wasn't able to slip past the guards and get out of the residence, he might not make it.

However it would be an honorable way to die.

In pursuit of vengeance.

"Memorize that code."

"Fine," she said. Man's most hated word in the English language when spoken by a woman.

"Repeat it back to me," he demanded. He wanted her to have a way out, not be trapped down here.

She did what he asked but she wasn't happy.

"Okay. It's been a pleasure, *chagiya*."

Barb grabbed his forearm. "Wait."

He could feel her nervous energy. For whatever reason, her worry had the opposite effect on him, and a fatalistic calm descended. He lied, "I won't be long."

She surprised him by bumping up against him and she gave him a short, soft kiss. Her lips clung to his as she pulled back. "For luck."

Before she could pull away, he canted his head and dove into a carnal kiss. Just in case this was the last time he saw her, he wanted it to be spectacular. Her hands were hot on his skin, her hips cradled his erection, and her scent surrounded him as he devoured her, just ate her up like her was inhaling a plate of spicy *Tteokbokki*.

Ken broke away from Barb and flashed her a cocky smile. "I don't need luck."

CHAPTER 7

With that parting line, Ken dragged himself away from the communications room and into the elevator.

Ileon jen-jang.

He'd been seconds from ravishing Barb on the Formica console of the secret bunker. He'd forgotten everything. Lost in the cocoa depths of her eyes, he'd had one thing on his mind and it wasn't avenging his father.

Or helping the people above escape those terrorists.

It had been her. What was it about her that made him lose all focus?

He needed to get his fucking head in the game, otherwise, he might not have a head.

Ken flipped on the monitors in the elevator, and wiped the sweat from his forehead. It was hotter than the surface of the sun in the elevator but at least he could see where the intruders were located.

The head terrorist was still in the ambassador's office with Choi's family.

Two were in the main reception area, still screaming at the hostages.

Another patrolled the back exit, one stood guard by the front door. And the last two were herding the kitchen staff into the main reception area to join the embassy guests.

Once they got the kitchen staff inside the large room, the two terrorists roamed the halls, continuing to search for anyone hiding. They were the unpredictable ones. And the ones he needed to avoid. He needed to hope the head guy was too busy beating the shit out of Soo-jin Choi to be diligently watching the security transmissions.

His best bet was the back entrance to the house. The territory the guard had to patrol was removed from the main party room. If Ken could get a jump on the guy without his buddies noticing, he could confiscate the comm device and backpack that all the guards wore. Then he could use their communication tools to try and get a message to the authorities.

He'd call Carson, or Jamie.

He wasn't a complete monster. He wouldn't just leave the hostages in jeopardy.

Ken observed the monitors, timing the guards' rotations. And he could go in five, four, three, two, one.

He eased open the panel in the ceiling of the elevator car. He wanted to leave the disabled elevator on the ground floor, he didn't want the terrorists to have access to Barb or that secret room. Especially since they seemed to want the same information he did.

Damn. The heat in the shaft was ten times worse than in the bunker. Ken quietly swung over to the ladder embedded in the opposite wall and began to climb.

Counting off the seconds in his head, knowing he only had five minutes before the guard would be in range of the elevator again, he quickly climbed to the first floor. Ken didn't want to alert the guard to the presence of the elevator if he changed his surveillance pattern. So instead of exiting the tunnel at the ground floor, Ken continued to climb until he located the air conditioning vent between the first and second floors.

Ken pictured the layout of the building in his mind, thinking about egress points and calculating where he would end up if he crawled through the metal tunnels.

He had to get this information out, which wouldn't happen if he got caught.

After figuring out which direction he needed to go, he headed into the air duct. He was able to slide into the metal rectangular tube without too much trouble. He slithered along until he got to the first air return big enough for him to fit through. Watching the hallway, he waited for the guard to patrol past him.

Good thing he'd grabbed that small toolkit.

With quick twists of the mini-screwdriver, he was able to open the vent cover. He gently pulled the grille into the air duct and stuck his head out for quick recon of the hallway. Empty.

He lowered himself through the opening and dropped to a crouch on the slick marble floor. He knew Barb could see him on the monitor, so he stared straight at the security camera mounted in the corner of the hallway and gave her a brash smile and a quick thumbs-up.

She was going to be pissed when she figured out he was leaving her.

He was almost sorry he wouldn't be around for the fireworks.

A silly smile spread over his face as he imagined her response when she realized he wasn't coming back.

So strange. He never smiled. And yet she'd managed to amuse him twice.

He needed to get out of here and quit thinking about the lovely Barb. She wasn't his concern anymore.

MY THROAT TIGHTENED, a hard knot of fear made it difficult to swallow. My heart rate was going haywire as Ken disappeared into the heating and air conditioning ductwork.

"How the hell did I end up here?" I muttered. "Go on a blind date, she said. Let down your hair, she said."

And fool that I was, I had grabbed on to that olive branch with both hands.

If I could see Jamie right now, I'd swing that branch and take her down. I smiled evilly as I thought about knocking Jamie Hunt to her knees. Basically trying to distract myself from what was going on outside this room.

Because Ken was in the vent system, I couldn't see him now.

I split my focus between the monitor that showed where I expected Ken to reappear and the activity in the main reception area. The terrorists continued to scream and rant at the hostages but hadn't really said what they wanted besides the ambassador, who still wasn't here. The rest of the hostages were cowering against the wall. My chest burned with the need to do something. Anything.

But right now I was trapped down here, waiting on my date.

Hydrogen, Helium, Lithium, Beryllium, Boron, Carbon. I listed the elements in the periodic table in order of atomic number trying to stay calm. *Nitrogen, Oxygen.*

Shit. I needed oxygen. *Breathe, Barbara.*

Objectively I observed the tremor in my hands from the adrenaline while I watched the monitors anxiously.

The terrorists were taking a particular glee in beating a man on the floor. They were yelling and I turned up the monitors, wondering if they were finally going to get around to verbalizing what they really wanted.

"You gutless coward!" the terrorist yelled. "Show yourself."

The more I studied the guy, the more I was convinced he was just biding his time.

"We know you are here. Quit hiding behind women and

children." Another yelled and unloaded his gun into the ceiling. The sharp retort of the automatic rifle was loud even in my little bunker. I couldn't imagine how loud the noise would be in the actual room. "If you come out, we will let all the hostages go."

Some of the hostages began praying. But their body language had relaxed. They weren't as frightened.

The gunman shot more of the ceiling. Several people screeched and clapped their hands over their ears, ducking their heads, trying to become as small a target as possible as chunks of plaster rained down from the destroyed and gouged ceiling.

The terrorist continued to shout, and he had an unholy glee in the crinkle of his eyes through the mask. Though it was difficult to tell, I thought he might be smiling.

It finally struck me what was wrong.

He knew the ambassador wasn't here. He was throwing the equivalent of a temper tantrum and beating the man on the floor for no reason.

Movement on another monitor caught my eye.

Ken emerged from the HVAC vent. He slowly peeked his head out but he was screwed if anyone noticed him because the thin metal wouldn't protect him from the deadly pierce of the terrorist's bullets.

My breath trapped in my lungs, and each thud of my heart echoed in my ears. In a purely acrobatic move he bent in half and lowered himself through the vent, moving slowly, but with extreme control.

Then he dropped to the stone floor and into a sinuous crouch, his movements precise and graceful. His formerly white wifebeater was smudged with gray, and his hair was mussed from traveling through the vents. He crept toward the rear of the house, moving with a fluid grace.

Then my heart stopped. The guy at the back of the house was moving toward Ken and Ken wouldn't be able to see the guy until the terrorist was right on top of him.

"Look out!" The warning burst out of me even though I knew it was stupid. He couldn't hear me.

With shaking hands I flipped switches, trying to find the one that would give me audio on the scene unfolding in front of me.

But as if he heard me, Ken flattened into a small alcove designed to display artwork, his silhouette nearly hidden by the indent in the wall. The guard was almost past Ken. For a moment I thought the guard was going to pass without noticing him. And then Ken would have had the tactical advantage, but he must have seen Ken from the corner of his eye.

He lifted his gun to shoot and all my blood drained to my feet. I swayed.

Oh shit. Oh shit.

But in some athletic martial arts move, Ken kicked out and the weapon went flying. I waited for a hail of bullets but there must have been a lock on the trigger because it fell with nothing but the clatter of metal onto the stone floor.

The fight was like a ballet. A hot, sweaty, choreographed dance of brutal kicks and vicious punches. I winced as one of the guard's kicks connected with Ken's ribs, but in a crazy acrobatic move, Ken walked halfway up the wall and flipped, using the guy's back as his lever so he didn't crash to the floor.

The only sounds in the hallway were the grunts as they fought with precision and intensity. The look on Ken's face was cold, predatory. Until Ken finally got leverage, hopped on the guy's back, curled his arm around the man's neck, and squeezed.

The guard whirled around, trying to shake Ken from his back. Ken's palm was wrapped over the guard's mouth.

The guard backed up and rammed Ken into a framed picture of a peaceful Korean rock garden. The photograph smashed to the floor, glass shattering, so very loud.

I held my breath, and my frantic gaze shot to the screens showing the other intruders. Thankfully it looked like no one had heard Ken's fight with the guard.

The guard had to be suffering from a lack of oxygen. But he wouldn't give up. He pulled a knife from a scabbard on his belt and swung the blade behind him.

Ken reared back to avoid the knife.

The guy overbalanced and fell backward. Ken jumped free and rolled to avoid getting crushed by the guy.

Ken's chest heaved as he jumped to the balls of his feet. He didn't even flinch when he landed on his bare feet in the shards of glass and waited for another attack. But the guy didn't get up, he lay on the floor.

What was he waiting for?

"Be careful," I whispered. "Be careful." What if it was a trap?

Ken waited for another minute before the sound of the other terrorists shooting at the ceiling in the main party room caused him jump into action.

He rolled the guy over and swore. The muttered "Fuck" grated over my ears like fingernails on a chalkboard.

Far too efficiently, Ken stripped off the guy's backpack, and grabbed his old-school walkie-talkie. Ken glanced both ways, then dragged the guy into the women's bathroom.

Realization hit. That man was never waking up. He wasn't unconscious. It was obvious why the guy wasn't moving now. When he'd fallen, he'd managed to impale himself on the knife he'd tried to use against Ken. The blood puddle on the cream marble floor was a dead giveaway that the guy was dead. The obscene smear of crimson on the shiny floor was a big fat clue.

I shifted my attention to the next monitor, trying to keep track of where all the intruders were located. I was trapped beneath a group of violent terrorists, now down by one, and over a hundred hostages, and no way to communicate with the outside world.

So far the gunmen had seemed to be randomly grabbing hostages and beating them, howling for the ambassador to show himself. But I was pretty sure they were only toying with the hostages while they waited for the ambassador to arrive.

Ken didn't even look in the backpack, instead he beelined for the rear exit.

For a moment, I might have panicked. *What if he leaves me?* I mean yeah, he told me how to get out of here if I needed to but he could have easily been telling me that so he could take off in good conscience.

Then I thought about who I was dealing with. He was a spy. He'd brought a blind date to a party where he clearly had an agenda and it wasn't to get to impress the girl and get to know her better. I was pretty sure he'd found what he'd been looking for. There'd been a moment, a mere blip of time, where his tension had minimized and he'd fiddled with his watch. His concentration on the one file had been extreme.

Panic fluttered in my heart as if finally hit me.

He wasn't coming back.

CHAPTER 8

K en refused to feel guilty.

For killing the guy or for leaving Barb. Yes, he was an asshole. Team Asshole at your service.

Shit. He felt guilty.

He slipped out the back door. Skimmed his gaze left and right. Before he could do more than take a breath, he heard a car approaching. The back of the house displayed the same attention to traditional Korean design as the interior. The landscape included plenty of native trees and a beautiful trickling stream from a fountain behind a rock arrangement.

Maybe Carson and the NSA had been listening to the transmission from the bug on his invitation. Maybe they'd alerted the FBI and they were here to save everyone.

He didn't have time to make it across the exposed cobblestone driveway to hide behind the garage. So he skulked around the back of a stacked stone altar and crouched behind the stone that depicted the square earth. The grass and rock-strewn area was frigid on his bare feet. His heartbeat throbbed in the ball of his foot where a cut from the broken glass oozed sullenly. From his position, he'd have an unimpeded view of whoever was coming up the driveway.

The garage door began to roll up.

Ken peered through the foliage at the base of the altar. A stretch limo came into view just as the garage door finished opening. The diplomatic plates gave away the limo's probable passenger. Ambassador Choi.

Damn but he'd love to let the guy go inside and get his ass kicked. But since the terrorists were heavily armed, Ken couldn't let Ambassador Choi go in there. He wanted the ambassador to feel the public shame of his actions. He deserved no less than what had happened to Ken's family in the aftermath of his father's death.

And since he didn't know what the terrorist's end game was, he needed to keep the ambassador from entering his residence. He couldn't afford for the ambassador to give the mercenaries access to the bunker. Right now Barb was trapped inside. Shit.

The limo stopped short of the garage.

The passenger window rolled down.

The ambassador's security detail was not happy. The guy in the front passenger seat jumped out. He unholstered his weapon and stalked toward the back door. "Hold on, sir. Let me clear the way."

But the ambassador was already exiting the car.

"I strongly advise against this," his security detail said. "Especially with a party in progress."

Before Ken could show himself, the ambassador raised a pistol, a giant fucking cannon. He shot the security detail in the back of the head, then spun around and shot the driver through the open window. Blood and brain matter splattered against the windshield in thick clumps.

What. Just. Happened?

The ambassador's actions were so surprising it took Ken a

minute to realize there'd been no loud sound. A silencer. The casual violence stunned him.

Most of his work was covert. Shadows and secrets were his weapons. Not bullets. Of course he'd killed people when he'd been in the army. But the ambassador hadn't even blinked as he'd blown away those men.

The ambassador's mouth curved into a satisfied smile and he sauntered toward the rear entrance of the house. The soothing, serene tinkling of the garden fountain was an odd juxtaposition to the extreme violence of the moment.

Ken shook off his inaction. He didn't know why the ambassador's cavalier attitude to death shocked him. The man had led the charge against peaceful protesters thirty-six years ago.

Ken ducked down to make sure that the ambassador didn't see him but the guy wasn't expecting anyone to be around and didn't even notice Ken as he entered the house.

Was the ambassador working with the terrorists? That didn't make any sense. There was no solid end game to him working with the mercenaries inside. Although Ken thought back to the Go Bag and the passports.

He could disappear. Have surgery to change his features. It was possible. But *why*?

Ken knew he didn't have much time.

If the ambassador was working with the terrorists, then he'd be sure to question why there hadn't been a man at the back of the house.

Ken hustled over to the guy on the ground. He had limited time to see if either of the men were alive. He bent over the guy on the dark gray cobblestone and checked for a pulse. He didn't expect one, but just in case. The rapidly spreading puddle of blood pretty much guaranteed the guy wasn't getting up.

Dead.

Ken scrambled to the limo and did the same with the driver. Also dead.

Fuck. He couldn't leave Barb in that house. He had to get back to her. He might be an asshole but even he wasn't enough of an asshole to leave her vulnerable in that bunker.

But he also had to get the photos of the files he'd taken uploaded to his online server.

He considered the views on the security cameras. Right now he was definitely out of range. He thought about where the security cameras were placed in the garage. The main camera was focused on the door that led into the house. So as long as he stayed away from that entrance to the house he should be fine. He headed into the five-car garage.

A catering van was parked in the bay closest to the door that led to the house interior. The battered van with a magnetic sign on the side advertising the catering company had been parked nose out. He peered in the open window. The keys were in the ignition. Ken reached in and grabbed the keys. Getaway car.

Then he prowled the perimeter of the garage, searching for any kind of communication equipment, a cellular hotspot or Wi-Fi box, making sure to keep clear of the camera.

He found the internet equipment box near the rollup door in the far left corner of the garage. All the lights were dark. They had disconnected and unplugged the box. Excellent. All he needed to do was reconnect everything and the system should reboot. Ken knelt down and opened the panel to the box. Ice blazed through his veins, cold like the burn of interrogation drugs.

They hadn't just disconnected the box. Plastic explosives had been pressed into every crevice until the box was full.

Fuck.

The terrorists were planning on blowing the garage. He had to assume that if they were blowing the garage, they intended to blow the house too.

Explosives were not his area of expertise but fortunately it wasn't a particularly fancy bomb.

No timer.

Urgency thrummed through his veins like a low level vibration buzzing with worry. He had to get Barb out of the damn house.

His hands were steady as he clipped the wires that would disable the explosive device. Then he'd go rescue his date.

With a small sigh, he removed his watch and set it on the shelf above the communication box, tucking it away behind a bag of tree fertilizer. Another element added to increase the explosion from the bomb?

Once the internet system rebooted, his watch would automatically upload the pictures he'd taken to his secure online storage account.

He had protocols in place. He had to log in to the account at least once a week. If he failed to log in, then the entire contents were to be sent to Carson Black. He didn't believe his handler at the CIA would disseminate the information. But Carson had to have some idea why Ken had wanted into the ambassador's lair. So, the contents would be delivered to Carson along with a note that requested Carson use the information Ken had collected to reveal the ambassador's treachery.

Ken didn't know if the terrorists were watching the monitors. He'd have to be ultra- careful when he went back inside the residence.

Once the reboot was in process, he headed back into the war zone.

He refused to consider that he wouldn't make it out. He'd spent his whole life working to avenge his father's death. To ensure his father's honor would be restored and that the man who'd been responsible for his father's death would pay. He couldn't fail now.

CHAPTER 9

The ambassador swaggered through the back door with a smirk on his face.

"No. No. No. Go back!" But of course he didn't hear me. And I didn't have time to climb the elevator shaft and warn the ambassador he was walking into a trap.

He stopped. Turned around. Frowned.

Strode forward. Stopped. Turned around again. The second time he faced forward, he spotted the smear of blood on the floor. Yes! He'd figure out something was wrong and skedaddle out of here and away from danger.

But he didn't leave. He shoved open the bathroom door, his head canted down, so I knew he was looking at the dead mercenary.

And again, instead of leaving, he slammed the door shut and stalked toward the main room. He wasn't worried or confused, he was pissed.

I didn't understand.

He pushed into the main party room and chaos ensued.

The terrorists grabbed him and started yelling, but I was pretty sure he wasn't surprised.

He wasn't flinching in fear. He wasn't wide-eyed at the destruction that had already taken place.

"What is going on here?" he demanded arrogantly.

"At last, the traitor to the people is here." A masked mercenary shoved the ambassador toward the room where they were holding his wife and son.

Again, he didn't appear upset or worried. He seemed way too accepting.

He stood beneath his family portrait. As I studied his posture and demeanor, something seemed off.

One of the guests stood, chest puffed out, his voice full of bravado. "You got what you want. Let us go."

"You have no idea what we want." The leader lifted his weapon and shot the man point-blank in the heart. Blood and tissue blobs patterned the wall as his body thudded to the floor.

Everyone screamed.

The terrorist cocked his head, shouted, "Anyone else?"

Oh shit. What was I going to do?

I wasn't some cowering damsel. My knight had abandoned me so I was going to have to fend for myself.

The computer hummed. I pressed the space bar and the screen came to life. My gaze went straight to the bars in the lower right corner looking for internet connectivity. And yes! Ken must have at the very least gotten me set up before he bailed.

What to do?

I thought about who had the most pull, then I figured—fuck it. Quickly, I typed in the email addresses for Jamie, Lucas, Stacy, Jordan, and Zeke. My pals from the NSA and the CIA. Hopefully someone was working and would see this.

Luckily I remembered their email addresses.

. . .

To: Jamie Hunt, Lucas Goodman, Staci Grant, Jordan Ramirez, and Zeke Hawthorne
    From: Barbara Williams
    Re: Hostage situation

"S.O.S. Hey long time no talk. I'm at the home of Ambassador Choi from the Republic of Korea. We've been overrun by terrorists. Approximately six, oops, no seven, that I can see. One terrorist dead. There are approximately one hundred hostages, some injured, one dead. The ambassador appears to be working with the mercenaries. Currently I am okay but a little freaked. So yeah, Jamie, thanks for the blind date. Your pal Ken left me. Anyway, help would be appreciated. Yes, that's an understatement." I added the urgent tag and pressed Send.

I thought about sending one to the FBI main email to report a crime. What were the odds that someone would read it and believe me?

With a glance upward, I said a little prayer and hoped that one of my friends would see the message. Fast.

Next up, I went to the duffel bag where Ken had found that envelope. With quick efficiency, I pawed through the bag until I found the manila envelope. I fanned through the pages wondering if I'd recognize anything.

The number 18 caught my eye.

I wondered if it had anything to do with May 18. I tried to scan through the papers but they were mostly in Korean, which I didn't read. But since I was pretty sure they were important I wasn't leaving them behind. Assuming I actually got out of here.

Which right now was not a given.

I awkwardly slid the manila folder down the front of my dress. Luckily the beaded bodice was tight enough that it should hold there. The paper was sticky against my stomach.

Why did he have to leave me?

Oh pity party, poor me. I couldn't wait to give him a piece of my mind when I saw him again. Whenever that might be.

And then I didn't need to wonder when I'd see him because Ken appeared on the monitor, coming back inside the house. The tension I'd barely acknowledged left my body in a whoosh.

He hadn't left me.

My relief was so profound that it hissed from me in a sigh.

But oh shit, what if they saw him on the monitors?

With determination he lifted the weapon he'd taken off the guard and shot out the security camera in the hallway. The corresponding security monitor screen went black.

Which helped him if the bad guys were watching, but also meant that I couldn't track his progress. Dammit but I hoped the other terrorists were too busy with the ambassador's arrival to notice that Ken was in the hallway.

There'd been a slight hitch in his step. While he might be annoying, and I was pretty sure he'd planned to leave me, I didn't want him hurt.

I stared intently at the monitors, knowing that if they saw him, I would be able to tell. Although what the hell I was going to do about it was another story.

Within a few minutes, he had made it back into the bunker room and I could finally let out a breath.

Now the hitch in his step was more noticeable.

So were other things. Gone was the suave, smooth operator who had picked me up at the Sofitel. His T-shirt was smudged with dirt, and sweat stained the armpits.

A bruise high on his left cheek marred the perfection of his face, and his hair stuck up every which way, no longer a perfect fall of silky black strands. His appearance was rougher, and my first thought was totally inappropriate.

Yum.

I was going to play it cool. "I didn't think you were coming back." My voice shook ever so slightly and I really hoped he hadn't noticed. So much for cool.

He looked at me steadily. "I wasn't." The dammit was unspoken.

Well, that was uncharacteristically truthful. Points for honesty.

He blinked and somehow I thought he hadn't meant to tell the truth.

"What happened?" Then I noticed the smear of blood on the floor. "You're hurt."

"I didn't know you cared."

"Shut up and sit down."

Ken dropped into the leather chair, and the lines of tension around his eyes were much clearer to see. "We've got problems."

I thought about what I'd seen on the monitor. "Yeah. I don't think the ambassador was surprised."

"I believe he's in cahoots with the terrorists," Ken said. He ran his tongue around his teeth. A spot of blood smeared the corner of his mouth. As his tongue probed his lip, I had the strangest urge to lean over him and press a healing kiss to the injury.

Before I could talk myself out of it, I'd bent and bussed his lips. So soft. So unexpected. My eyes closed and I savored the intimate contact. When his tongue met mine, I melted. The caress was light, sweet. So different from his hard demeanor that the dichotomy called to me.

That impulse for tenderness was a surprise. His response even more so.

His fingers tightened on my hips, but then he loosened his grip and eased away from me.

"What was that for?"

I shrugged, turned away so he wouldn't be privy to the swell of longing that broke over me. "Let's get you cleaned up."

I retrieved the first aid kit from the storage cabinet and

rummaged through, looking for antiseptic and bandages. Once I'd found them, I opened my sequined little purse and pulled out a small bottle of hand sanitizer and rubbed a generous amount on my hands before touching him.

Ken subdued a groan as I lifted his foot to my lap. "Does it hurt?"

His soft mouth had quirked, not enough to show his dimple. And his black eyes seemed to lighten. "I'll live."

Suddenly his amusement wasn't quite so funny. He hadn't meant to kill the man. I knew that and still… "Are you okay?"

He knew exactly what I meant. "I'm fine."

"But—"

"Consider it another black mark against my soul," he tossed out flippantly.

"Really."

"Look, *yobo*. In the pursuit of democracy for my country, I've done many things that skated the line between good and evil."

And I had the unerring confidence that he was trying to convince himself, not me.

"He would have killed you," I said.

Ken raised one eyebrow. "Darling, if you're trying to comfort me, I can show you a much more pleasurable method," he purred.

Dick.

I flushed. That's what I got for trying to be understanding.

BARB EFFECTIVELY EVADED his come-on and bent her head to probe the cut on his foot. Her posture caused the beaded V neck of her dress to gape open, just slightly, and expose the swell of her breasts. Even though he knew her intention wasn't to tempt him, his body responded accordingly. For a second, he thought she was going to take him up on his flirting. A move meant to distract. He didn't actually think she'd go for it.

But his body was on board.

"Let's get that fixed up."

The attention was uncomfortable. His skin prickled and felt too tight. "It's fine."

"Let me take care of it."

No one took care of him.

From the time he was a baby, after his father died, he'd been the man of his family. His mother had admonished him that his task, his purpose in life, was to avenge his father. She'd insisted Ken follow the revenge path before he even understood what revenge meant. But she'd impressed on him that to bring honor to their family, he must achieve his goal.

"Really, you don't need to do this."

"Don't want an infection." Barb gently clasped his foot in her hand. Her fingers were cool and soothing against his skin, her hands gentle as she probed the wound. "No wonder you're limping. There's a piece of glass in there."

She leaned closer, her breath puffed against his arch, and his body stood up and took notice. His cock, which had been ambivalent to female companionship lately, perked up. Again. She was so close that when she looked up from examining his foot, she was going to get an eyeful.

Instead of worrying about it, Ken sat back and appreciated her body.

He didn't have time for more than a one minute fantasy. The terrorists clearly had an agenda. They needed to get a message to the FBI. And he needed to figure out how to get a call out to Carson. Pronto.

Barb was carefully extracting the glass from his foot. And he was engrossed by the valley of her cleavage. The urge to bury his face between her spectacular breasts and breathe in her essence was a distraction.

He needed to focus on their more immediate problems, but right then and there he made a promise to himself and her.

"When we get out of here, I'm planning on drowning in you. I want to find a bed and not get out for a week."

She flushed, a subtle blush moving up her chest and into her face, but didn't look up from her doctoring of his foot.

"I've got to get you out of here."

"Me?"

He hesitated.

"Oh hell no." She fisted her hands, propped them on her hips, and glared at him. "You are not keeping shit from me."

His gaze flicked to the monitors. "What have I missed?"

"Beatings. The ambassador arrived and was not surprised." Barb spread antibiotic ointment on the cut, the brush of her fingers so light that the touch was barely there. "Do you have any idea what's going on?"

"I don't." It was true. He had no fucking idea what was going on.

"Who are they?"

Ken shrugged. "Speaking French and English. Their body armor is state-of-the-art and their armament is likely Chinese. They move like Korean special forces." Hopefully she wouldn't ask how he knew that.

And he still had no fucking clue what they wanted. She finished by pressing a square bandage over the cut.

Ken flexed his foot, testing for any restriction or pain. Not that he had the liberty of indulging in reduced activity if it hurt. "Thanks for the field treatment," he said as he stood.

She nodded curtly.

"Don't worry." He pacified her. "Just go ahead over there—" he gestured to the large leather chair beneath the safe, "—and I'll get you out of here as fast as I can."

The verbal equivalent of a pat on the head. *Go be a good girl and shut up.*

79

He just happened to glance at her and see her eye roll.

"Are you honorable?" she asked abruptly.

Her question took him aback but he didn't have it in him right now to be evasive. And he wasn't sure that she wouldn't call him on it if he was. "Of course."

Ken wasn't used to women like her.

His dates tended to be either clueless hot women who were down to fuck and provide some fun in bed or other operatives who were aggressive and horny and looking for carnal relief. They didn't last and they didn't matter. But what she thought about him…mattered.

It shouldn't. She shouldn't.

Yet he found himself wanting to reassure her that he would not let her down.

There was a solemnity to the moment that seemed warranted. Ken executed a little bow, "You have my word." In that moment, he knew he would not let anything happen to her. But she didn't strike him as the type to be passive.

The type of date he'd been looking for. Not too bright, not too inquisitive.

He thought he'd known what he needed. He'd been wrong.

"Okay, then please let me help."

He still kept quiet.

"I helped Jamie with a few sensitive situations and I never told a soul. You can trust me."

He couldn't trust anyone. But her plea compelled him. "We need to figure out what these assholes really want." He grabbed the backpack and opened it up.

The first thing he tossed on the counter were two off-white rectangular blocks that looked like putty. "Shit. I hate it when I'm right."

"Is that…?" Her eyes were wide, frightened.

"C4."

"Explosives?" Her voice cracked. Her pulse thundered in the base of her throat.

Ken dropped his head forward. "There's enough here to blow the entire residence. But the bag is missing the charges that would be needed to detonate this amount of C4."

"Not particularly encouraging."

"Understatement," he muttered.

"So that's good then? No charges?"

He figured he'd keep the presence of the explosives in the garage to himself. "I need to get you out of here." He continued to pull items out of the backpack.

Energy bars. Gatorade. "Looks like they planned to settle in."

The temperature in the small bunker had risen. She wiped her forearm over her forehead, and the sweet scent of her perfume floated between them.

"Why'd you come back?" she asked softly. "You could have left and gotten help."

"What kind of date would I be if I abandoned you?" His words were flippant. But he meant them. He likely should have taken that van and hightailed it out of here. But he couldn't leave her at the mercy of the terrorists.

"I attempted to reboot the Wi-Fi. We need to see if it worked."

The determination to come back had been tempered by the worry about Barb.

She had somehow gotten under his skin. He hated that she'd been a distraction, even as he knew his humanity was on the line. He should have left and gotten in touch with the American authorities. But he hadn't. Instead he'd come back into this quickly escalating situation to save her.

Her mouth lifted, drawing his attention to her lips. To the promise of paradise.

Ken shook his head, shook off the surprising attraction to her. Paradise would be revealing the truth to the world about what really happened during the Gwangju Uprising. Not losing himself in the wonderland of her body.

At the bottom of the backpack, a paper bag rustled.

He unrolled the top and opened the bag. The smell hit him. Decay. Blood.

He peered inside. Everything in him stilled as he catalogued what he was seeing.

A hand. A human hand.

Severed from the rest of the body. A plastic baggie was rubber-banded around the cleanly sawed wrist bone and splattered with blood.

Ken gagged as he pulled the hand out.

Barb turned around from putting away the last of the first aid supplies.

"Oh my God." Her horrified gaze shot to him. "What would they need a hand for?"

CHAPTER 10

Anoise from the monitor drew Ken's attention to what was happening upstairs. He needed to get Barb the hell out of here.

The ambassador was ranting about hurting the boy. "This was unnecessary." He waved his hands toward his son and paced back and forth.

"You are in no position to make demands." The terrorist got in the ambassador's face but there was something off about their interaction. As if they were putting on a play.

Meanwhile the ambassador's wife was slumped in a wing chair by the fireplace, blood trickling down her temple. She hunched to the side, her fingers curled as she cowered from the intruders. The ambassador had barely assessed her for damage, but now he scowled at his wife.

"Have you no honor as a mother?" The ambassador backhanded her and she whimpered. "Give them what they want while I attend to my son."

He yanked a *pojagi* from the wall and knelt to wipe the blood from the boy's face.

Alarm bells were going off in Ken's head. Not so much that the man would be worried about his son but the fact that he was trying to clean his wounds with a family heirloom.

The ambassador Ken had known would never desecrate that fabric.

Choi valued the old ways, as evidenced by the plethora of treasures spread throughout his house.

"Give us the code to the secret room." The head terrorist prodded the woman with the barrel of his assault rifle.

The ambassador flicked his gaze to his wife and nodded.

"I don't know it," she wailed. Tears leaked from her swollen eye as she pleaded with the guys with the guns.

"Give it to me or I'll shoot your son." He pointed the weapon at the teenager lying on the floor.

The ambassador threw himself in front of the boy. "No."

Ken raised his brows. "That's not right."

"Which part?"

"The whole scenario. The boy should be protecting his mother." Ken narrowed his gaze at the scene taking place above them. "That should be his duty at all costs."

"Not the dad?"

He shrugged. "I wouldn't know. My father…died when I was a baby."

She traced her index finger over his tattoo. The number 18 overlay the Korean symbols for May on his biceps. As if she knew what the date meant to him. How it had shaped his life. A reminder, a penance, to never forget the massacre and what happened to his family.

His heart clenched. A weird unexpected reaction to her touch.

"Is this why you don't know?" she asked softly.

He captured her fingers to stop the gentle caress. "Yes." Her hand was delicate—unexpected since she was such a force—but not fragile, strong in his.

"What does it mean?"

"It's a reminder."

"For what?"

"Never forget."

The leader was pointing his assault rifle at the wife.

"They'll do it." Barb shivered despite the fact that the temperature in the room had risen steadily. Sweat covered both of them.

Ken tilted his head. "Why isn't *he* giving them the password?"

"How did you know it?"

He hesitated. "A friend."

Barb pursed her mouth. He tried not to react to the pucker. He knew she hadn't intended for it to be sexual but his brain went to other things she could be doing with her mouth.

"It changes every day," Ken said thoughtfully.

He glanced around the small room. Noted details that before had only registered at the periphery of his thoughts. "Huh."

"Am I going to get more clarification?"

"The cherry blossom branches are a few days old." He took that into account and added it to the slightly stale air when they'd first come down here.

"So you think he hasn't been in here in a few days."

He bent and studied the slightly browning pink petals. "Several."

"We need to get out of here," Barb whispered. "Before they get in."

"I disabled the elevator."

"Oh and that will stop them, just like it stopped you." Barb rolled her eyes. "You got what you came for. Let's get out of here."

He raised a brow.

"I'm not stupid," Barb said. "And it looks like our friendly terrorists are looking for the same thing. Access to this room. Access to these files."

On another screen, two of the terrorists were dragging the dead guy from the bathroom. They flipped him over then ran back in the bathroom. Muffled shouts penetrated as they came back out and kicked their dead comrade.

"They're freaking out about the backpack." Ken's smile was dirty, happy.

They had their walkie-talkies and were communicating with the main guy. The terrorist diverted his attention from the scenario in front of him and turned his back on the ambassador and his family.

"What do you mean it's missing?" He shoved over a ceramic urn. The crash was loud as the pottery shattered on the slate floor. "We need what's inside."

He swore creatively for several seconds.

"Find that damn backpack." He tossed the walkie-talkie on the desk. "And figure out who killed him."

He turned back to the ambassador and his family.

"My patience is gone," he roared. "Tell me how to get into the basement room."

"It is my husband's secret room." She jerked her thumb toward the ambassador. "Ask him."

Everything finally clicked.

Holy shit.

He grabbed the hand gingerly and headed for the safe.

"Oh my god. What are you doing?" Barb's face blanched.

"I need your help." Ken popped open the door to the safe. "We need to get the entire palm pressed against the infrared reader."

"But—oh, shit." She glanced back at the monitor. "You think he isn't the ambassador?"

"Yes."

"How?"

"Could be his double. That's pretty common. Maybe the guy

up there had plastic surgery as an official double or he's altered his appearance to impersonate the ambassador."

"It's like I'm in an alternate reality." She scrunched her face at the sight of the amputated hand.

"Don't be squeamish."

"Dude, I'm a molecular biologist. I'd wager I've had more experience with cadavers and body parts than you." She shuddered. "At least I hope so."

She'd handled the past few hours with grace under pressure. "Why aren't you afraid?"

"Of these guys? Believe me, I'm shaking in my boots." But she'd held it together so far.

"Why aren't you afraid of me?"

"Lucas would never set me up with someone he thought would hurt me," she said softly.

Ken swallowed at the pure affection in her voice as she was so sure that Jamie's significant other wouldn't hurt her.

"Let's get this done. Find out what is in this safe that is so important."

Which had to be what the terrorists were after. Why else would they have had the severed hand in the backpack?

They held the hand up to the glass screen and watched the scanner check the dead palm print against the stored print. With an anticlimactic click and a pneumatic hiss, the door swung open.

Barb's bare arm was pressed up against his, their skin slicked together, heightening his awareness of her closeness and her scent, which should have faded but had only gotten stronger in the heated room.

Ken tucked the severed hand back into the paper bag.

Barb squirted hand sanitizer onto his palm and hers. Cringing with disgust, she rubbed the alcohol gel over her hands while Ken did the same.

Then he turned his attention back to the safe and let out a

long slow breath. He'd already found what should have been the ambassador's most private files. What could be in this safe? Duplicates?

"So we're in the ambassador's private room with special access," Barb said. "And we just opened his super-secret safe with a biometric reader."

"That's affirmative."

"Yikes. So the ambassador is…."

"Dead."

CHAPTER 11

I t was like I was trapped in some bizarre punk'd play.
   I needed Jamie and Lucas to jump out and laugh and say,
"Gotcha!" Except there was nothing funny about this day. I'd
kept moving so the fear couldn't overwhelm me. And yes, I felt
removed from the violence, huddled down here in this relatively
safe haven.

But if those terrorists were able to get down here, we were
trapped.

Ken had emptied the safe, which held only a bit of money, far
less than what was in that bag, and two USB flash drives.

"Shit." Ken shoved the money into his pocket and clutched
the USB sticks in his hand. "Whatever is in on these drives must
be more valuable than the antiquities scattered around
this room."

"Information?"

He paused, cocked his head. "Likely."

"We need to find out what's so important." Ken was already
at the computer setup. "What could be more significant than
what was in the Go Bag files?"

He plugged both drives into the computer and clicked on them waiting impatiently while they loaded. The first drive blinked as he inserted it into the USB port.

A list of files appeared on the screen.

The first stick contained files in Korean. At least I assumed it was Korean. I couldn't read it. He skimmed through the file folders quickly.

"What's on the other drive?"

When he clicked on the second drive, it was a list of file names. In English. One caught my eye. "May 18. That sure seems to be popping up regularly."

His biceps, the one with the tattoo, flexed.

Before he could react, I clicked on the file.

I scanned the contents. "According to this file, the US government had willingly withdrawn their troops, knowing that the new Korean government intended to use force to subdue the protesters." My breath caught.

Ken hadn't moved. He barely breathed as I read the file contents out loud.

"Fuck," he grated out. He pressed his palms flat against the console, and hunched toward the computer.

I guess that indicated how he felt about the US government putting diplomatic relations over the lives of Korean citizens.

"What does this mean?"

"Betrayal," he whispered.

I wrapped my arms around his waist and leaned against his back. I had seen his face in the reflection of the computer screen. He'd been unable to conceal his devastation, telling me everything I needed to know.

"I'm sorry."

Ken stiffened beneath my embrace.

Then he turned around. He nuzzled my neck, nipped his way up to tug at my earlobe. I tilted my head back to give him access. His mouth captured mine. With a gentle lick, he caressed my lips.

He exhaled, his sweet breath huffed soft against my cheek and shivered over my skin.

"Once we're out of here, I want to fucking devour you."

I loved his positive thinking. But how the hell were we going to get out of here? "If we get out of here, I'll let you." My fingers and toes tingled with a cocktail of adrenaline and fear.

The lead guy was in the Ambassador's wife's face. "Take me to the damn elevator."

Her expression was stoic. Her attitude pure Korean rage but no distress showed on her face.

When the bad guy grabbed her arm, only her eyelids flinched. I clutched Ken's biceps, my nails dug into his bare arm, his skin hot and smooth against my palm.

"Are they going to kill her?"

"Not before she leads them to the elevator."

What would happen if they found us?

Ken studied their actions. The leader murmured something to one of the masked people in the room. Then the person headed for the hallway that led to the rear of the building.

"Here we go," Ken murmured.

"We're going to have to force it," the lead guy snarled.

The woman jumped up, half bent over, she kept bowing at him until he jabbed her with the barrel of the assault rifle.

The wife gestured with her hands for him to follow.

I wondered if now was the time to mention that I'd grabbed the manila envelope with the file on May 18.

"So something on these flash drives is what they are looking for."

Ken closed the flash drive folders on the main screen and quickly pulled them from the desktop tower. "We don't have time to figure it out now." He clutched the drives in his fist.

I tried not to panic but his urgency was catching. "What do you want me to do?"

"We need to get a message out and then get the hell out of

here." His urgency transmitted in his sheer stillness. The calmer he got, the more I could feel my anxiety rising.

Ken continued to listen to the intruders.

"I already sent a message."

He grabbed me, held me captive as he cupped my cheek with his callused palm. My knees literally went weak. "You brilliant, gorgeous woman."

I flushed. It wasn't that I was unused to compliments, it was that I didn't think he was used to doling them out. I didn't melt. I was tough, I was cautious, even in my personal relationships. A result of my upbringing and the need to fight for every single positive event in my life.

Ken broke away. All business again. "Check and see if anyone has responded."

But the internet was down again. "It's not functioning. Stupid computers. Why couldn't the internet access have a backdoor?"

"Backdoor, backdoor." Ken kissed me, lingering against my mouth. Then he pressed a single gentle kiss at the corner of my plump lips and pulled away. "Jesus, you are a genius."

"While I appreciate the sentiment, what in the sweet hell are you talking about?"

"The ambassador hadn't stayed in power because he was stupid. The asshole had a contingency for his contingencies."

"Backdoor." I got it. "You think there's another way out of here."

"Yeah."

"Does it make sense to leave the bunker?"

"Based on the contents of that backpack, we've got to take the chance." Then he muttered, "Maybe Jamie did me a favor."

"Yeah, Miss Pliable and Not Too Bright would be freaking out right now." I smiled. Why had Jamie set me up with him? "How do you really know Jamie?"

"I told you, we dated."

I snorted. I knew he was being evasive. "No way she'd give up control for you."

Ken asked. "What makes you say that?"

"Have you *met* Jamie?"

Once again, I surprised him. And he grinned, those unexpected dimples making an appearance.

"Point taken." Ken sobered. "It's classified."

So, work. They had worked together. I don't know why that brought me such satisfaction, but I hated the idea that he and Jamie had kissed, or more.

"But you still can't tell me what's really going on *here*." With you. Frustration prickled me.

"I…can't."

The sense of disappointment was overwhelming. But we didn't have time to dwell on it because the damn terrorists were getting closer.

"Okay. Here's what we're going to do." He quickly outlined his plan.

"Not crazy about leaving you behind." I flattened my lips and my gaze pierced him with a fierce intensity. "Use me."

My mind immediately went to a few ways he could use me but that wasn't what I meant. His mind went to the same place, if his smirk was anything to go by.

I slapped his shoulder. "Focus."

"Did you just…smack me?" An uncharacteristic laugh burst out of him and highlighted those dimples.

How could I not be attracted to the little dip that peeked out when he really smiled?

"Yes." I sent him an answering smile.

The ruckus on the screen drew our attention again. We couldn't see what they were doing because Ken had shot that camera. Not being able to see was worse. We could hear them. Choi's wife had shown them the panel. The clang of metal as they tried to open the elevator doors echoed in the suddenly silent bunker.

"We've got to get you out of here," Ken said.

He pressed the lever to reveal the hidden room where we'd found the bag. Ken stepped into the darkened interior. I grabbed the lantern and turned on the light so we could see.

"When you said backdoor, it made me realize he had to have another way out of here."

"And you think it's in here?"

"I think it's awfully odd to have this space with only a single bag in it." He was running his fingers along the wall. I held the lantern high so he could see.

"Found it."

Just in time. From the monitors, we heard the bangs as they shot at the elevator doors. That wasn't going to work.

"Get the explosives," the leader growled. "We're going to blow it."

"Time to get out of here."

The interior of the small storage space swung outward, revealing a tunnel. He handed me the flash drives. "Put these in your bra."

If the situation hadn't been so dire, I might have teased him. But worry had my stomach flipping and my heart racing. Ken slung the assault rifle he'd taken off the guard around his shoulder. He unzipped the duffel bag, grabbed the shoes and tugged them on his bruised and bloody feet.

With the exception of a slight tightening of the skin around his eyes, he didn't react to what must be painful. If I didn't know, I wouldn't have had any idea that his feet were hurt.

Ken ushered me through and then he slid the storage panel door shut, so even if they explored, unless they knew to look for a hidden room, they wouldn't find us. At the very least, it gave us extra lead time.

Ken ran his fingers along the seam of the wall and pushed.

The wall swung outward and revealed a tunnel. He pulled me through the entrance and then quietly closed that door. The tunnel immediately illuminated with lights where the walls met the ceiling.

He held his index finger to his lips and mimicked "shh."

He grabbed my hand and led me through the tunnel. His fingers curled around mine, his touch reassuring. I wanted to crowd closer, to press up against him for comfort.

His wifebeater T-shirt was stained, blood dotted his back. "You're hurt."

I hadn't even thought to look at his back when I'd been tending to his foot.

He shrugged. "Not the first time."

I couldn't believe my first impression of him had been of a pretty boy without substance.

"Let's get you out of here."

What about him?

The tunnel forked. "Which way?"

He stared at the two options. "Pretty sure if we go left we'll end up under the garage, which would be the logical exit point."

We went left and at the end of the tunnel was a stairway.

"Where do you think it leads?"

"Only one way to find out." Ken pulled me along quickly.

The stairs seemed to go on for more than a single level but finally there was a light at the end.

When we got to the doorway, Ken pushed me back against the wall. "If my sense of direction is correct, we're coming out at the garage, which is perfect."

I didn't want be a Negative Nellie but we didn't have ride.

As if he heard my thoughts, he pulled a ring of keys from his pocket and dangled them in front of me.

"What are those?"

"Keys to the catering van."

I wasn't going to ask.

"Once we get there, it's got to be quick."

My heart thudded. "Hopefully they won't be watching."

"They wired the garage to blow," he said reluctantly.

My breath caught. "What?" Then why the hell were we headed to the damn garage?

"I disabled it. But—"

"Holy shit. Why didn't you leave?"

"You were still here."

His confession struck me in the solar plexus. "You...came back for me?"

That thought melted me. Just made me want to collapse into a puddle of pure emotion. He hadn't left me. He'd come back.

Holy shit. That was pretty epic.

CHAPTER 12

K en needed to get Barb in the van and get her the hell out
of here.

He poked his head out of the access door, searched the
garage quickly, looking for enemies.

"Looks like it's clear." He handed her the keys. "As soon as I
give the go-ahead, you get in the van and get it started."

A sense of urgency pulsed beneath his thoughts.

He had the proof that Choi had instigated the deadly force
against the protesters during May 18, and maybe even evidence
of corruption, and the revealing evidence that the US
government was complicit in the deaths of all those citizens, plus
whatever else was on those flash drives.

The international and diplomatic repercussions would be far-
reaching.

Not to mention the repercussions for him personally. But he
couldn't think about that right now. Couldn't dwell on the
shocking information. Couldn't dwell on the fact that both of his
governments had betrayed his family.

Ken wanted Barb out of here. Safe.

He hustled her to the van. They didn't have much time. Especially if the mercs were watching the monitors.

"Come on, *chagiya*." Ken boosted her up into the seat and quickly shut the driver's side door.

"Um, Ken?" Barb had twisted the keys in the ignition but her gaze was glued to the rear view mirror.

"You've got to get out of here."

"We've got a little problem." She hiccupped.

He jumped up onto the runner, leaned through the open window, and pressed a kiss to her open mouth. "Trust me there's nothing little about it."

"Jokes? You're making jokes right now?"

"Laugh or cry, babe."

"Well, he's too dead to do either." She jabbed her thumb toward the cargo area of the van and the corpse that lay on the floor.

Ken slid the back panel open. He hopped inside to double-check, scenarios running through his brain as he calculated odds. "There's one mystery solved."

"Not very sanitary to have a dead guy in the back of a catering van," she quipped but her voice was shaky.

"You've got to get out of here."

"With the dead guy."

"You already had his hand," Ken muttered as he stared at the mostly frozen corpse of Ambassador Jung-ho Choi. "That was enough to get you into the safe. Assuming you could get into the secret room. What did you need Choi's body for?"

Possible reasons flitted through his mind as he prowled along the garage looking for any other surprises. None of the scenarios he could come up with spelled anything but disaster. The explosives, the Ambassador's body.

"If his body is in this van and they had wired the garage to blow, they wanted his body to be discovered."

She was too smart for her own good.

"Yeah." Fuck. Which meant they weren't planning on survivors.

Because if Choi's dead body was in this van, frozen and on the way to thawing, they damn well wanted his body discovered in the aftermath of the hostage situation.

The body positively confirmed that the guy who looked like the ambassador actually wasn't him. So who the hell had been on that podium an hour ago standing next to the President of the freaking United States?

Was the president in danger? Thinking about how close the president had been to an imposter, one who didn't have South Korean and US relations as a priority, as far as he knew, had him breaking out in to a cold sweat.

The imposter could have done a brush pass with a slow-acting poison. If these terrorists had been intent on destabilizing world order, and destroying United States and South Korea relations, killing the president would be an excellent method.

The terrorists clearly didn't want the fake ambassador to be discovered. The only people who would know that the guy on television wasn't the real ambassador were the people in this house. If any of the party guests suspected, to keep that a secret, everyone here had to die.

"Get to Jamie." Ken commanded her. "Give her the evidence we recovered."

"Where are you going to be?"

"I can't let them get away with this."

"But—"

He was behind the driver's seat. "We don't have much time. My guess is someone saw us on the monitors. I need you to get out of here."

He pressed a kiss to her cheek. "Be safe," he murmured in Korean.

He hopped out of the van and slammed the door shut. "Go."

The limo was still where he'd left it but the dead agent who had been lying in the middle of the cobblestone driveway was gone, only a puddle of drying blood remained, and a smear that indicated someone had dragged the body somewhere else.

Her chocolate-brown eyes shimmered with tears. "Be careful."

"Hell of a first date." Ken smiled and slapped his palm on the side of the van. "Go."

She peeled out in a squeal of tires and the smell of burnt rubber. Just in time as three of the mercs ran out the back door and headed straight for them.

One turned, dropped to a knee, and raised his arm to shoot at Barb.

Barb swung the van in an arc and took the guy out. He hit the grill, then flew through the air and landed with a non-recoverable thud, even as one of the other mercs started shooting at the van.

Ken dove for the limousine, using the chassis and the fortified wheels for cover.

"Hey," Ken yelled. He shot a burst of semi-automatic rounds toward the asshole shooting at his girl, drawing his attention so she could get away. The spent casings pinged on the stone as they ejected from his weapon.

Fuck he'd forgotten about their state-of-the art armor.

"*Gaejasik*," snarled one of the soldiers over the sound of rifle fire. "You're dead."

Finally, he had confirmation. *Gaejasik*. Motherfuckers were Korean. Yeah. But no fucking way were they going to harm a hair on Barb's head.

Their automatic fire rocked the limo as the rounds hit the armored car. Air hissed as a round pierced one of the tires. Another bullet skipped along the cobblestones and ricocheted off the ground before hitting his ankle.

Shi-bal, that hurt.

But Barb was gone.

If nothing else, he'd saved the girl and gotten the proof out. Which should have made him happy, but he realized he wanted more. He wanted her. And fuck him if after years of being focused only on revenge was he going to be denied the chance for peace.

CHAPTER 13

The van careened down the cobblestone driveway through the tunnel of cherry blossom trees. The pink-petaled branches blurred.

"*OmiGodOmiGodOmiGod.*" I'd hit that man. Yes, of course I knew that he was going to shoot at me. Try to kill me. But, "Oh my God."

The thunk of bullets hitting the back of the van revved my heart again and I pressed the accelerator to the floor.

"Huh, huh, huh." I tried to draw in breath but my lungs were tight, as if a giant had wrapped its fingers around them and squeezed until my heart was beating so hard that I thought it just might explode in fear. Tears streamed down my face, my neck, and followed the beaded edge of my dress until the salty water pooled in my cleavage.

"Get hold of yourself, Barbara." I gripped the steering wheel with clammy fingers.

Tried to calm my thoughts but my brain couldn't settle on one thing.

Freaked that I'd hit the guy with the van, terrified for Ken fighting the guys with weapons, horrified at the information we discovered, worried for the hostages.

Where did I even go for help?

Jamie. Ken had said, get the information to Jamie. Which was fitting. She got me into this mess. She could damn well get me out.

I whipped onto the winding road that led to the highway and immediately slammed on the brakes. The unwieldy van went into a fishtail. The road was blocked with police cars, Humvees, emergency response vehicles, ambulances, pretty much every kind of law enforcement you could imagine.

I skidded to a stop, tires burning. The van screeched as it rocked to a halt.

Guys dressed in SWAT gear circled the panel van, standing far enough away that I didn't hit anyone. Every single shooter had their weapon raised and pointed straight at me.

"Oh my God." I raised my hands, praying. "Don't shoot. Don't shoot."

"Step out of the van slowly." Someone on a bull horn directed.

Jesus, I was going to go into tachycardia if I didn't slow my heart rate down. "I'm opening the door," I called through the open driver's window. I pulled the silver handle and the door creaked open. I pushed it wide, conscious of the multitude of weapons pointed at me.

With my hands up, I slid awkwardly off the raised seat until my bare feet hit the cold asphalt. Shit, my eyelashes were clumped from the tears coating my cheeks. A shiver shot through me as I stepped away from the open doorway. I could barely stand my body shook so hard.

My teeth clattered as reaction from the adrenaline froze me.

The booted, armed soldiers ran up to me, weapons steady. One cuffed my wrists behind my back with plastic zip ties, the restraints tight. While another frisked me, sliding his hands up my legs until he was at the juncture of my thighs. I had the random thought that he'd gotten further than my date.

Oh my God. My date. Ken was still back there.

I was on the verge of tears again.

Hopefully the men who'd been shooting at him hadn't hit him.

"Who are you?" A bull-chested man in khaki pants, a navy polo shirt, and a dark blue windbreaker with big yellow letters spelling out FBI on the back approached me with a harsh expression on his face.

"You need to get to the ambassador's house. They're holding the guests hostage. You need to help them," I urged him.

"Who are you?"

I wasn't important. "They have explosives. We think they're planning on blowing it up."

"Who are you?" He was right up in my face, shouting, spittle from his mouth hit my cheeks.

"Barbara Williams. I was a guest, but the people still in the house are what's important."

"How'd you get free?"

"My date." Helplessly I glanced back at the house, barely visible through the trees. Was he okay? Our connection had been forged in the fire of shared camaraderie and adrenaline-fueled kisses. My heart ached with the possibility that he was hurt or worse. I turned back to face the angry man who had not backed down at all.

Troops, SWAT, police mingled around the van.

"They killed the ambassador."

"That's impossible," Angry FBI guy said. "He was just on television making a plea for the terrorists."

"The guy on TV is a fake."

"How do you know that?"

"Because the real ambassador is in the cargo hold of the van." I tilted my head at the vehicle. Jesus, did this guy not get that the terrorists were holding many hostages in that house? Why was he so focused on me?

"Did you kill him?"

"What?!" He needed to focus on the damn point. Idiot. "They've got hostages. They have already killed several people. You need to save them!"

A bald black man in his mid-fifties dressed in a nicely tailored gray suit and a geometric pattern silk tie hustled over to us. He patted my shoulder and smiled at me, then directed his attention to the man yelling at me. "Back off, Harold."

"Black. What are you doing here?"

Black? As in Carson Black? So this was Jamie's boss?

"She's…with me." He placed a gentle palm on my shoulder. "Someone get those cuffs off."

"You can't do that."

"She's the one who alerted us that the hostage situation was in progress," Carson Black said with exasperation.

Within a few moments, someone had handed him a pair of box cutters and he efficiently snipped the flex cuffs.

"Thank you." I rubbed my wrists but kept my gaze trained on the driveway to the house. "Sir."

"Call me Carson, dear." His smile was gentle, regretful.

I knew he was Jamie's boss. And Ken was familiar with him. Had even wondered if I was working for the man.

Which meant he was dangerous. But right now he felt like the older brother I never had.

FBI guy barked out, "If I find out you had anything to do with this—"

"Harold, if you want to have a pissing match, let's wait until we get the party attendees rescued." Carson Black's voice was snippy. "Any other intel?"

I thought about the flash drives digging in to my breasts and the scratchy papers tucked between my body and the tight bodice of the dress.

Now that the FBI was here to rescue the hostages, I wasn't giving the information to anyone but Ken.

Somehow, forged in the last few hours, he'd earned my loyalty and my trust.

"Barb, dear, if you have any information on the terrorist's playbook, you need to share it with us, so we can make sure the hostages are safe and the right side wins," Carson said softly.

I wasn't sure I wanted to share because it occurred to me that if they knew about the C-4 they might wait to breach the house. But Ken was in there. So were the other hostages. "They have explosives."

As if the Universe heard me, a small boom rent the air.

The house was still standing but the entire structure seemed to shimmy on its foundation and then settle back down.

My heart stopped.

The FBI guy ran toward the Humvees, walkie-talkie at his mouth as he directed the SWAT members to move in. It was a small explosion. The house was still standing. There were no screams.

That was all good news. Right?

CHAPTER 14

J *en-jang.*
That explosion came from inside the house. They must have blown the elevator doors like the leader threatened. That definitely meant Ken didn't have much time.

He was still pinned down behind the limo.

The car was leaking fluid, and the radiator hissed with warning. The only other sounds in the suddenly silent air were the rack of the slide of their weapons and the heavy breathing of both his opponents. As they reloaded, Ken ducked down and shot at one guy's ankles. It was a difficult shot but that small opening between suit and shoes was one of only a few vulnerable spots on the expensive body armor, unless the damn bullets were armor piercing.

A hoarse shout told Ken he'd scored a hit, and the guy's body thudded as it hit the ground. But he wasn't dead. Huh, armor piercing. Which was good for him and very terribly bad for him.

As the guy rolled around swearing, Ken bent and took one more shot.

And fuck him, in a lucky shot, he hit the back of the guy's

head. His skull exploded, spewing blood and brain matter all over the cobblestones. If these rounds could pierce that expensive fucking armor, he was in deep shit. They would slice through his skin and tissue like a samurai sword through silk.

There was still one more terrorist left and he was swearing at Ken with a creative mix of Korean and English. He couldn't leave the cover of the limousine so he needed the last guy to come to him.

And quickly. Because with the amount of noise they were generating, it wouldn't be long before more mercs came running.

The sound of a round being chambered alerted him that the last guy was on the move. Ken rolled under the limo toward the other wheel well. Once he was situated behind the rear wheel, he flipped open the Cold Steel Tiger Karambit knife in his left hand and waited for the asshole approaching to give him an opening.

Ken watched the last guy's movements, shooting randomly in the wrong direction to throw him off. If he timed it properly he could take the guy down. He had a small window of opportunity and a limited amount of space to maneuver underneath the car. It was a gamble if the guy approaching the limo decided to check beneath the car, but Ken had to go for it. His weapon would never out-fire the assault weapon this guy was carrying. These fuckers weren't messing around.

Ken rolled into position, stifling a groan at the stabbing pain in his ankle. He'd live.

He waited, and sure enough the guy came around the trunk of the limo and stopped. He didn't know where Ken had gone. In that moment, Ken swung with a powerful arc and sliced the guy's Achilles tendon. Down the guy went, folding in on himself before arching back.

Ken shot a double tap to the heart before the guy could even lift his weapon.

He took a moment, breath heaving, relief and pain zoomed through him. But he didn't have much time. He stripped off his undershirt and wrapped his damn ankle, twisting the fabric and then tying it in a knot to stem the bleeding. It hurt like a bitch, but worst case he'd only chipped a bit of bone. He didn't think anything was broken.

Ken hopped up, checked all three guys, swooped up their rifles, slinging the extras over his shoulder so they hung down his back. Like a fucking Korean John McClane. He cautiously approached the rear entrance to the house, hugging the wall, waiting for discovery. Waiting for the bullets to start flying. Again.

Shit.

He was tired. He'd prefer to be headed to Barb's hotel room, to enjoy the pleasure of sex with her, a physical connection on an ephemeral plane rather than going back into the den of thugs who had taken over the ambassador's house. He was tempted to just...go. But he couldn't just leave the terrorists or the hostages here.

He crept inside and paused at the destruction. The false sliding panel that had hidden access to the elevator had been torn from its track and lay crookedly against the opposite wall.

The result of the boom was clear: the elevator doors had been blown open. Puffs of smoke drifted in the air, filled with the smell of explosives, and gunpowder stippled the reinforced titanium doors.

They hadn't been built to withstand explosive charges set directly on their stress points. He peered down the shaft. The hatch in the elevator car's ceiling lay open.

The ambassador's wife, Soo-jin, was propped next to the door, her head canted at a dead angle. Her eyes stared vacantly at the smear of blood on the marble floor that he'd incurred what felt like a lifetime ago. Ken knelt to close her eyes, and planned his strategy.

First, get the hostages out of the house.

Then, go after the fake ambassador.

By his count there were only two terrorists left up here. He'd killed three, Barb had killed one. That left two in the main room and the leader and the fake ambassador in the bunker below.

He sent up a little prayer of thanks that Barb was gone with the evidence they'd found. Hopefully she was safe.

He crept toward the large party room and hoped his assumptions were accurate. The house was now sweltering. Sweat poured down his face and coated his torso. His ankle hurt like a bitch, and he had a mental clock ticking in his head.

According to the chatter on the walkie-talkie, the mercenaries had notified the FBI that there were hostages. He knew they were planning on blowing the house, so by his estimation he had limited time before the feds were here and the house went up in a massive explosion.

But first they had to find what they were looking for. Ken didn't plan on them getting their way. He stopped at the arch into the party room. The hostages were lying on the floor face down.

Several were weeping softly.

The two guards patrolled the room in a crisscross pattern, which meant for about thirty seconds they were within a few feet of each other.

They weren't expecting an attack.

If he timed it properly, he could take out the two guards in a one-two burst of gunfire. Several more hostages had been shot. One lay groaning on the floor.

"Shut up," the guard yelled.

Ken waited until the two guards were within a few feet of each other and distracted by the injured man, who hadn't stopped moaning. Then he opened fire, shooting the one facing him first. Before the other could turn around, Ken shot him in the back.

All before they could get a warning to the guys in the bunker.

Hostages were screaming, wailing.

"Everyone up," he yelled as he ran toward the two terrorists to make sure they really were down. "The house is wired to blow. You need to get out of here."

The floor was a moving mass of people as the formerly elegant and wealthy guests scrabbled to their feet and sprinted toward the door.

"Jesus, Park." Dick Herring hobbled over. A thick trail of blood ran down his temple. "You okay?"

"I'll be fine. Can you make sure everyone gets out?"

"Yeah. Where are you going?"

"To get the terrorist leader and the ambassador."

"Don't start an international incident with the ambassador."

He figured now wasn't the time to tell his boss that the real ambassador was dead. But he could clue him in that things had already blown past the incident stage. "Yeah. Based on the demolished elevator and dead partygoers. Too late."

Dick shooed him away. "I've got this."

Ken ran for the elevator. He needed to access the basement bunker. ASAP.

Fuck. He quickly climbed down the ladder inside the elevator shaft, trying carefully not to make any sound. Then he peered through the hatch of the elevator roof and carefully assessed the situation inside the bunker.

He'd estimated correctly. In the bunker room were the merc leader and the imposter ambassador.

What he hadn't counted on was their hostage. Fuck. The ambassador's son was slumped on the chair, clearly he was injured, not dead. But Ken had to tread carefully or the teen could end up dead.

"Can you blow this?" The fake ambassador was examining the safe.

"I have some C4. We had to conserve." The leader had removed his mask and tossed it on the console by the computer setup. His move confirmed that he was also Korean. "Who the fuck killed my guys?"

"And stole our damn access." The fake ambassador slapped his hand against the safe door.

The leader set the charge on the safe quickly and efficiently. "The better question is where is he now?"

In less than thirty seconds, the mercenary had effectively damaged the safe but they still weren't able to get inside.

"Do it again," the fake ambassador insisted.

The leader twisted his wrist, looked at his tactical watch. "We've got to get out of here." He flicked the dial on the walkie-talkie and tried to raise his men.

But they didn't answer, because Ken had killed them.

"Fuck." He shook the communication device. Tried again.

Ken assessed his options. He needed to stop these two but he also had to assume the kid was their insurance.

While both men had their backs turned, he quietly lowered himself to the floor of the elevator car. Crouched behind the wall, he waited for the right time to strike.

They were both still too close to the kid to attempt to take them out.

The leader set another charge. The loud pop did the trick but still didn't rouse the kid in the chair. The safe door hung crookedly from its hinges.

The imposter ripped the door off, then started cursing.

Because Ken and Barb had taken everything, and presumably the guy had come for whatever was in that safe.

"*Shi-bal.* That fucker took the flash drives." The imposter kicked over the small table with the ashtray and the vase with the cherry blossom branches. "And God damn Jung-ho. Even in death he's screwing me."

He dropped his head and took a deep breath.

The merc leader was yelling at the fake ambassador as he shoved the artifacts into a large duffel without care for their value or fragility.

"We can't take those." The fake ambassador shook his head.

"Fuck you, Jim," the leader snarled. "We don't have much time and thanks to you we didn't get our meal ticket. The blackmail potential supposedly in that safe was my retirement."

"It wasn't just about money."

"It was for me." The merc leader dumped the last treasure in a bag he must have brought with him.

The fake ambassador reiterated, "We can't take them."

"Why the fuck not?"

"Because then people will know someone from the house made it out alive." The fake ambassador was swearing under his breath. "When they sift through the rubble the rescue workers need to find those objects or at least pieces of them. They need to know that Jung-ho double crossed the Smithsonian and the Republic of Korea and kept the original treasures for himself."

That was one mystery solved.

And fuck. Ken hated being right. They were going to blow the house. Hopefully Dick had gotten the hostages out.

His only consolation was that he was pretty sure they didn't have any intention of blowing up themselves with the house.

The fake ambassador brushed a gentle hand over the boy's head. "We need to go." He hefted the boy over his shoulder.

"I'm taking these." The military leader was frantic, lugging the bag with the artifacts toward the closet while the Jung-ho imposter pressed the button to open the door to the tunnel.

"I can't let you do that." The doors swung open and the imposter held up a detonator, his thumb pressed down.

The leader stopped. "You can't blow me up, asshole."

Ken crouched in the corner and readied to launch himself. He had to get to that detonator before the fake ambassador let go. Or they were all dead.

SECOND-GUESSING SUCKED.

After not telling Carson about the flash drives, my conscience started to protest. I huddled in a corner arguing silently with myself about handing over the evidence Ken gave me. Hopefully he'd escape soon and he could deal with disseminating the intelligence to the right people.

Before I could move past that thought, Jamie was there.

"Holy shit, Barb." Jamie panted. Since I knew she was in damn good shape, she'd clearly run a long distance otherwise she wouldn't be breathing hard. Bizarrely she was wearing one of those big blue windbreakers with the yellow FBI letters. But I knew better than to ask why.

"You know I didn't make the connection when I put you two together, but I realized later you're Barbie and Ken."

"You set me up," I hissed. I was still pretty annoyed with her.

"True." Jamie tapped a finger against her mouth. "How'd it go?"

"Really?" I waved my arms toward the mass of emergency personnel. "How does it look like it went?"

In a totally uncharacteristic move, Jamie giggled. "On my first date with Lucas, I was bugged, drugged, and kidnapped." She snickered again.

I still only knew the bare minimum of details about how they met. "That wasn't a date. It was a hookup." I rolled my eyes.

"Yet he followed me across the country." Her voice had softened. "And here we are, a couple years later, still together."

"How is he?"

"He's…good. Great." Her smile was radiant, happy, and lit up her entire face.

"That's good." And it was good. Huh. The familiar bite of jealousy that typically hit me when I thought about Lucas and Jamie together was absent. An odd and welcome warmth filled my chest. "I'm glad."

And I was.

I was positively thrilled that Jamie and Lucas were together and happy. Not even a twinge of sadness.

Suddenly, the front door to the house burst open. People started pouring from the ambassador's residence like rats abandoning a sinking ship, screaming and pushing and shoving as they spread out over the lawn and sprinted down the driveway.

"Hold fire," Harold shouted. "Hold fire. Let them get away from the house."

Ken must have been successful. My eyes filled. "He did it," I whispered.

Carson Black stood on my left and Jamie on my right as we watched.

"We're going to have words," I told her. I still might kick her ass. "You set me up," I said again, because dammit it bore repeating.

"On a date." But her eyes were sparkling as if the world had played a giant cosmic joke on me. "So how'd it really go?"

I wanted to fume. I wanted to blast her for the amusement and irreverence. But, I realized that while the date had been unconventional—to say the least—I liked him. If I was honest, I really liked him.

"I'm hoping it's not over yet," I grudgingly confessed. "You crazy bitch."

Jamie watched the battered and shell-shocked guests head to the ambulances parked up and down the street. "I'll take that as a win."

She was smiling.

And I smiled back. "Yeah. I won."

But as the last of the guests trickled out, Ken wasn't among them. Where was he? The boom of my heart accelerated rattling my ribcage.

"Shouldn't he be out by now?"

SWAT had surrounded the house and were slowly advancing. Red and blue lights from the fire trucks, ambulances, and cop cars flashed in strobe patterns, highlighting the protective guards that covered the officers' faces.

I held my breath.

Where the hell was he?

"Hey, he can take care of himself." Jamie tried to placate me. But her brow was crinkled, which was when I started to worry. She wasn't moving from my side.

Hurry. Hurry. Hurry.

Dammit I wanted him safe. Urgency pulsed as I waited. Someone draped a blanket over my shoulders but I couldn't seem to get warm as I watched the scene intently, a sick worry roiling my gut.

A horrific boom rent the air. The house disintegrated in an explosion of wood and slate and fire.

The SWAT guys flew through the air, lifted off their feet from the percussive blast as the rest of the house fireballed.

"Shit," Jamie mouthed. Or maybe she yelled it. I couldn't actually hear anything. She didn't move. Didn't react beyond that single word and yet I could feel her fear, her grief.

My eardrums were ringing. Light blinded my eyes as my brain fuzzed and the world spun. As a result of the blast or my fear, I didn't know. Ken hadn't come out of the house before it blew up. My legs crumpled and I fell to my knees watching, waiting.

The house and the garage were a smoking pile of rubble. The medics ran to triage the officers.

Horror, grief hit my chest like a sonic boom. Pain filled the gaping wound where my heart should be as I wept. Harsh sobs ripped from my chest, burning my throat and lungs, as I screamed. "Nooooo."

I realized I was clutching Jamie's arm so tightly my nails dug into her flesh. "He could still be in there. Right?"

But no one answered.

Carson knelt down beside me. "No one survived that," he

yelled. Carson dropped his head as if unable to look at me. "I'm sorry."

Paper, detritus, the remnants of the once elegant house floated down like gently falling snow on a winter's night.

The air was thick with smoke and ash. Noise edged back into my hearing. The wail of sirens, the roar of the fire hoses as firefighters attempted to extinguish the shooting flames.

"He died a hero." Carson wrapped his arm around my waist.

Cold enveloped me like I'd been filled with liquid nitrogen, my body rigid, yet fragile. With those few final words, my heart shattered into a million little pieces.

"I know you just met." Jamie curled her palm around my biceps, as if to help me up. "But he was a hell of a guy."

She had no idea. I gripped her wrist, holding on too tightly and I knew it. "You don't know." He was a hell of a guy but for so many more reasons than she would ever know because I was not about to betray his trust. To betray him. "You don't even know."

In a few short hours, Ken Park had gone from being no one, an insignificant date on a random night, to filling my whole world.

My legs refused to work. I just knelt on the ground, the stones from the street cutting into my knees, and mourned.

CHAPTER 15

God, he was one giant fucking ache.

And he was pretty sure he smelled. He couldn't tell because his nose was still filled with dust and ash from the explosion. He'd grabbed a slightly used white dress shirt from his gym bag in the back seat of his mostly destroyed BMW. Streaks of soot smeared his face, and his hair was gray with dust. He'd tried to clean up a bit in the ground floor bathroom of the Sofitel before going on this breaking and entering jaunt.

His car had been almost a total loss, but he'd found their phones when he'd gone looking for some clothes. Thankfully, her hotel used the new smartphone keyless entry so he had Bluetooth access to her room with her phone in his hand.

Carefully, quietly Ken jimmied the door to Barb's hotel room.

If hotel security cameras caught him before he could get inside, they'd have him out on the street in seconds. Finally, the damn lock clicked, and he let out a sigh of total relief.

He should have gone home, taken a shower, fallen into bed, and come to see her later.

Or he should have just returned her phone via FedEx with a

note that said thanks for a memorable evening. And stayed away from her.

Instead, he couldn't wait another second to see Barb. To touch her and make sure she was okay. To reassure himself she was unharmed.

Right now he just wanted to wrap her up in his arms and hold on tight.

The only place he wanted to be was here. The big question was…did she feel the same?

The room was darkened, only a trickle of light from the bathroom illuminated the area. He walked cautiously toward the bed. When he got there he knelt down and just stared.

She lay on her side, tear tracks on her face, her palms tucked beneath her cheek as if she were praying. She had kicked off the covers, revealing a cherry blossom pink lacy nightgown and matching sheer lace panties. Her dark chocolate and cream skin gleamed in the low light. And once again he was struck by how gorgeous she was. He skimmed his gaze over her looking for injuries. Looking for any hurts he could kiss better. She seemed to have survived their ordeal without any visible signs of injury.

Finally, the tension he carried eased. She was alive, okay.

She shifted on the bed and it occurred to him that being here in her hotel room before letting her know he was alive was a bit stalkerish. He didn't care.

Now that he was here, he was unsure how to wake her. "Barb," he whispered. "*Chagiya.*"

Still squatting on the floor, he lightly brushed his hand over her shoulder.

She shot awake, sat straight up in the massive king-size bed, eyes wide and filled with terror. Shit. He hadn't intended to scare her.

He slapped his palm over her mouth before she could scream. "It's me. It's me." He repeated the words in her ear until she stopped struggling.

119

Barb curled her fingers around his wrist and ripped his hand away. "You—" She threw her arms around his neck and launched herself at him.

He hadn't braced for impact and they tumbled to the floor in a tangle of limbs.

"You're alive. Oh my God."

She squeezed him, her arms circling so tightly he could barely breathe, and he didn't care. He lay beneath her, savoring the press of her body on top of his, the soft pillow of her breasts, and the hard ridge of her pubic bone against his rapidly growing erection.

She was solid in his arms. The scent of some flowery lotion had softened her skin making him realized how dirty he was.

Even though she appeared to be happy to see him, suddenly his urgency to get here seemed premature and awkward. What if that incredible connection he thought they had was really just a product of adrenaline and fear? So he blurted out his first random thought. "I should take a shower."

She wrinkled her nose.

Things got even more awkward, hesitant. She pushed her torso up and off his chest, staring down at him. Her body gleamed in the low light, her breasts nearly spilled from the sheer pink lace. And he wondered if he'd made a major miscalculation.

"You are looking a little...scruffy."

That was an understatement.

She had a secret smile and she nearly glowed with an inner light. "Good thing I like scruffy." She leaned down and gently pressed her lips to his. Her kiss soft, as if she was afraid she'd hurt him.

The brush of her lips was light, barely there then gone. But the contact was the reassurance he needed.

"Is that so?"

"Mmm-hmm." Barb lips curved.

"Is there anything else you like?"

Another smile, more sultry than the last, flowed over her face. But then she lost that flirty look. "Oh, I have your stuff."

"My stuff?" That was a weird segue. As in, time for him to go?

She pushed up until she straddled him, her knees outside his hips. The flirty pale pink lace skimmed the top of her thighs and lovingly cupped her breasts, dipping low to reveal a shadowed valley between the mounds. The precarious position made it impossible for him to move. He hoped she didn't notice his monster erection.

Barb pulled open the little drawer on the nightstand that held the requisite Bible. She removed a manila envelope and the flash drives, then handed them to him.

"What is it?" He hadn't looked at it, just concentrated on her.

"The papers you found in the bag, then put back, and the stuff from the safe."

His watch was gone. Blown up in the garage. He hadn't checked to see if the information loaded to his server. He'd come straight here.

The rescue workers who had pulled him out of the rubble wanted him to go to the hospital, but after getting the major wounds taken care of by EMTs, he'd left the blast site against medical advice and headed straight to Barb.

His need for reassurance that she was unharmed had pinged beneath the surface like sonar.

"You kept it?" He'd told her to get it to Jamie or Carson.

Barb shrugged. An embarrassed quirk to her lips, she cut her gaze to the evidence. "I knew it was important to you. And I...it was all I had left of you. I couldn't let it go. Not yet."

Her confession struck him dumb.

She lifted her gaze, the expression in her eyes a blend of defiance and embarrassment. "Silly, huh?"

That was when he knew. She felt it too. This odd bond that had already withstood so much and not broken.

Fuck, he wanted to just devour her, but he was filthy. Confidence and peace settled him. "I need to take a shower," he said again.

He held her gaze, staring into her glittering brown eyes as understanding sizzled. "Is there something you want me to do about that?" she teased.

Ken tossed the intelligence she'd handed to him onto the nightstand, discarding his life's work without hesitation. "Share it with me."

Oh my God.

Ken Park was alive!

And in my shower.

He'd stripped off his filthy pants and oddly clean white dress shirt without an ounce of modesty, revealing his muscular physique. His arms, his abs, even his thighs were sculpted works of art. All those muscles and definition had been hidden beneath a loose-fitting suit.

His formerly perfectly gelled hair stuck out in all directions. The slightest of scruff surrounded his mouth in a skim of black, outlining his soft lips. The single bruise high on his cheekbone reminded me that he'd been battling combatants just hours ago.

A gray ash coated his hair and skin. Then he pushed off his briefs, and I lost my breath.

His cock hung low and thick, the impressive length exquisitely framed by a small thatch of black curls. My mouth watered. My body sizzled.

When he noticed my stare, his cocky smile made an appearance. "You just gonna stand there?"

I was still out of sync. I wasn't regularly so hesitant. I had a healthy confidence about my body, but even so, stripping in front

him, this man who should be nearly a stranger, was bold even
for me.

Then his eyes warmed. "I'll be waiting."

He opened the door to the elegantly tiled shower and stepped
inside. The steam concealed him almost immediately but not
before I had a view of his most excellent ass.

All that lust buzzed through me again. Louder. Stronger.

This beautiful man was here. In my shower. Not dead.

And waiting on me.

With a happy sigh, I pulled the lace baby doll pajamas over
my head and shimmied out of the matching thong.

I inhaled, holding my desire in, and opened the door.

He was under the spray, his back to me, his biceps flexing as
he rubbed water through his hair. The sight of him struck me in
the solar plexus. He turned, eyes still closed as water ran down
his face, his head tilted back, the long column of his neck flexing
as he swallowed. How could a neck be sexy?

Yet it was.

He grabbed the soap and began rubbing the bar against the
rippled abs of his stomach. I was mesmerized by his lazy strokes.
My fingers tingled with the need to touch him.

His cock had filled, standing at attention. He opened his eyes,
his gaze catching mine. He stood across the large shower and just
stared at me as he curled his palm around his shaft and
soaped up.

The steam filled the air, heavy and expectant with need.

"Damn, you are stunning."

His words drew my attention from where he touched his body
to the desire shimmering in his eyes. I was a confident modern
woman who owned my sexuality but something in his look made
me pause because it wasn't just sexual.

It was…reverent.

"What?"

"Trying to convince myself that you're real." He reached out to me, his fingers curling around my wrist, and tugged.

I tumbled against his slick chest. His erection prodded my belly. My body flushed, and my head went woozy, as desire sent all my blood careening to my sex. That rush nearly brought me to my knees. He spun us around so my back pressed up against the cool tile wall, his front covering me.

I couldn't wait any longer to touch him. I flattened my palms at his waist, stroked over his ribs, his pectorals, and down his biceps, each glide confirmed that he was here, and mostly okay.

He nuzzled my neck, and the slight scrape of his beard set off tingles throughout my body. My nipples peaked, my heart pounded, and my sex softened.

"I am very happy to see you."

"How?" The question had been burning at the back of my mind. But I was so thrilled he was alive that I hadn't pushed but now I really wanted to know.

"How happy?"

"No. How are you here?" I forced the words through my tight throat. No one thought he had survived. "I watched the house explode. It was raining debris, ash."

"Ah, yeah. I was lucky." Ken rubbed his hand over his hair.

"How lucky?"

"I was in the elevator car when the house exploded. The titanium reinforced box withstood the initial blast and kept the rest of the rubble from falling on top of me."

My heart nearly stopped. He could have died. Should have died. "It's like the Universe gave you a second chance," I said softly.

Ken nodded.

"What about the fake ambassador?"

"Presumed dead. They were still looking for his body but he was in the tunnel when the house exploded."

"So it's over?"

"They still need to identify who exactly the imposter was."
Ken dragged his tongue along my jaw. "But yes, for you,
it's over."

Gratitude overwhelmed me. He could have died.

Warm water cascaded over us as I wrapped my arms around
his torso and squeezed. His little grunt surprised me.

"What's wrong?"

"Nothing."

Easing away from him, I took stock of his condition.

My breath stalled in my chest. His body was a mess. I bussed
my lips gently over the bruise on his cheekbone. His eyes drifted
closed at the gentle caress.

I skimmed my fingertips over the curve of his neck, stopping
at the large purpling bruise on his shoulder. "What happened
here?"

He opened his eyes, turned his head to look at the contusion.
"Falling debris from the explosion."

I shuddered. With a butterfly touch, I lightly brushed my lips
over the hideous bruise and then another kiss over the mark on
his ribs from the fight with the guard.

Carefully, I turned him around. Little cuts marred his back
and biceps. "Here?"

"First guard fight. My guess is when the glass on the picture
broke."

With sure moves, I pursed my lips and kissed each scar, each
mark. There were so many. I rested my forehead between his
shoulder blades and just breathed. Gratitude expanded my heart
like helium filling a balloon, and I gave silent thanks that he
was alive.

I turned him back around gently.

Then dropped to my knees. I skimmed my fingers over his
barely fuzzy muscular thighs and down his calves, until I saw the
bandage at his ankle.

"Here?"

"Ricochet," he ground out.

His voice had gotten grittier with each gentle touch. I knelt on my heels and bent over to press a kiss right above his anklebone.

I'd been so intent on kissing his hurts that I'd missed the bigger picture. But the evidence was right in front of me.

"This hurt too?" I leaned forward to kiss the head of his erection.

He reached for me, but I captured his hands and pressed them against the tile wall.

"Let me." The submissive position was out of character but I didn't care. I wanted to pleasure him. "You deserve this." He'd saved all those people. He'd protected me when he could have disappeared. He was a caretaker. A protector.

Right now, I wanted to take care of him.

I leaned forward, my palms against his thighs, then slid my hands to his sex. I cupped his balls in one hand and held his thick erection in the other. He was smooth, hard, hot in my palm and throbbed with life. Closing my lips over the bulbous head of his cock, I sucked him in, his salty male taste like an elixir on my tongue.

My heart was a mix of desire and profound thanks for this second chance.

Closing my eyes, I savored him. He filled my mouth, and I curled my tongue around his plump cap. With sure strokes, I swallowed, savoring the primal satisfaction as I took him deep in my throat.

He surrendered to my touch. His hips began to move in rhythm as I worked him. Loved him.

A tortured groan rent the air. "Fuck. Stop." Ken eased his cock from my mouth with a small pop.

"Fuck? Yes. Stop? No." I smiled against his erection, then dragged my tongue up the impressive length.

He pulled me to my feet. His rough palms grabbed my ass

and rocked me against his erection. His cock, hot and thick, pressed against my belly and my knees dipped. "I want inside you."

Perhaps I should have protested but I wanted him inside me too.

He hustled me out of the shower, cranking the water off. He lifted me up on the countertop and stepped between my spread thighs.

He nipped my mouth, his teeth scored my lips. That bite of pain shivered through me in a wave awakening nerve endings.

He scraped his hands over my flesh, palmed my breasts and squeezed. My nipples tightened at the erotic pressure and my body slicked, readying for his invasion. For him to take and give.

He groaned again. "Condom?"

"Bag," I gasped.

"Yes!" He lifted me up, his muscled arm around my back, the other under my ass.

"What are you doing? Put me down." He was going to hurt himself.

But oh my God, he was strong. And the visceral thrill I got from being the recipient of that strength and those muscles weakened my knees. Ken staggered through the bathroom door.

"I don't want to let you go." He tossed me on the bed and dove for the bag with the condom.

CHAPTER 16

K en wanted to inhale her.

He found the condom, rolled it over his cock.

Barb sprawled on the rumpled white cotton sheets. Her lithe brown body shimmered with little beads of water. "I just want to lick you up."

Her waist dipped in, one leg canted so he could see the lips of her sex, swollen and aroused, peeking from the thick nest of black curls. Her breasts were big enough to bury his face between them and play. Her hard nipples were a dusky burgundy, begging for his attention.

But what caught him, what turned him on the most was her air of pure sexy sweetness. Lush burgundy mouth tilted in a sensual smile, desire flushed her chest and face, and brightened her deep cocoa gaze with wanton abandon. "Who's stopping you?"

He thought back to when he'd picked her up for their date less than fifteen hours ago. He'd been annoyed and prickly. He'd wanted arm candy.

But she was so much more.

Smart. Sexy. Funny. *His.*

"Remind me to thank Jamie."

"Please don't bring up Jamie while we're having sex." But she laughed uninhibitedly and her breasts jiggled, drawing him to her with a powerful magnetism.

"Good point."

He crawled between her legs, taking time to kiss his way up her calves and thighs. Skimming his tongue along her inner thigh, he then reached the crease where her leg met her hip. He nipped at her hipbone, sucked at her soft fragrant skin, marking her with a dark bruise. Then he kissed his way down to her pubis bone until he hovered over her clit. Anticipation held him in thrall.

"Don't get shy on me now." She rocked her hips into his face.

"Just...savoring." He lapped at her sex, taking care to play, to nibble, to suck until she was writhing beneath his mouth. He pressed a little harder, rubbed the stubble from his beard against her swollen mound.

"Holy shit." Barb yanked his hair, then begged. "Inside me, please."

He wanted to devour her, just eat her up and shove her over the edge into orgasm. His whole life he'd lived in darkness, in shadows. But she was light.

He burned with the desire to take her in, to love her. To gorge on that light until it scorched him.

She rocked her hips urgently. Demandingly. As if she knew what was best. Ken smiled against her sex.

He curled his arms around her thighs, held her down so she couldn't pull away. He dragged his nose along her skin, letting her essence invade his senses. She squeezed her thighs around his head impatiently.

Laughter bubbled up. "Is that supposed to scare me?"

"Years of Pilates, dude." The tender skin of her legs rubbed against his beard. "I can crush your head like a walnut."

"Impressive." He pretended to give her what she wanted, lifting away from her body as if to enter her.

But he wasn't ready to give in. He placed sucking kisses in a line from her sex to her belly button, savoring the taste of her skin with each swirl of his tongue.

The sweet musk of her arousal drifted in the air.

She scraped her fingernails along his scalp, and tilted his head so their eyes met. She was fierce. "Please."

She tried to bat her eyelashes and pretend submission. But the demand came through loud and clear.

He kissed his way up her body slowly. "Years of Tae Kwon Do have given me great discipline." He smiled against her breast, then sucked the bud of her nipple into his mouth. She was tight, hard against the pull of his tongue. A fierce satisfaction flooded him as she arched into the intimate kiss.

"And I'm very happy for you." She rubbed her slick sex against his latex-covered erection. Even through the barrier, her heat seared him.

His cock swelled, harder, bigger. And his control broke.

Ken slid his arms beneath her body, cupped her gorgeous ass in his palms, and on the next upswing of her hips, he gave her what she wanted. What they both wanted.

Her body welcomed his as if they'd been made for each other. Like coming home. She was everything.

Once he slammed inside, his control broke. He lost his finesse, his skill and banged into her. He tilted her hips and hit her g-spot with every thrust. She wrapped her legs around his thighs, her heels digging into his ass, as if she was trying to absorb him inside her.

Her breasts bounced against his pecs, her nipples stabbed his chest, and her fingernails dug into his back.

Her channel gloved him as if she'd been created just for his cock. They were wrapped together in an intimate dance, each rock of their hips, his balls slapped against her swollen sex. His blood boiled, sweat slicked their skin, and their combined musk rose between the heated, sensual slide of their bodies. The need to celebrate life a melody that pulsed and flowed in the sultry air.

She bowed as her orgasm hit.

Her channel milked him in long hard pulls as she contracted around his cock. Ken grunted as his orgasm plowed through him with tsunami force. His vision dimmed and his heart thundered as he expelled his semen in hard jets.

Beneath him Barb continued to rock. Her sex fluttered around his cock. Until she arched back, eyes closed, her face a study in ecstasy.

His orgasm seemed to go on and on. As he emptied himself into her sex, he began to fill with joy, expanding until he thought he would explode from the wonder of it.

He collapsed on top of Barb, his breath heaving harder than when he'd been digging out of the rubble of the destroyed house.

Their hearts thundered in synchronicity.

He tucked his face into her neck, overwhelmed with sensation, and…feelings.

Peace. Home. Contentment.

Love.

And wasn't that a frightening thought.

Jen-jang. Love?

Sweat sheened her face. In the filtered light from the bathroom she glowed.

Ken rolled off her. Higher thought function returned. He'd taken her in the missionary position. And his stamina had been shorter than optimal. "Not my most creative effort."

They lay on the bed side by side. She was sprawled out, legs wide, arms open, the picture of relaxation and satisfaction. She turned her head so she stared into his eyes.

"Worked well enough." Her smile could light up the entire room. She patted his head condescendingly. "I'm sure you'll do better next time."

He wanted to laugh with her but something held him back. He propped up on one arm, his head in his palm, and traced his fingers along the curve of her waist.

She stopped laughing. "What's wrong?"

"Not a thing."

"But?"

He considered her question, but didn't speak.

"This is a surprise. You seem unsure," she prodded.

"Truth?"

"Yeah." Her voice was breathy.

"I've never cared enough for someone to have my performance matter."

She rolled and mimicked his pose, facing him. The light from the bathroom gleamed on the mounds of her breasts. She took his breath away.

There was a melancholy air to her smile. "I thought I did once."

"And?"

"Wasn't even close to what I feel right now."

It could be the forced intimacy and the heart-pounding rush of the life-or-death situation they had faced together. Caution was his method in everything. "It's possible that the feeling is just the result of adrenaline."

"Chemical reaction to the endorphins released during our adventure?" She cocked her head, considered his explanation. "Could be."

Except he had been in adrenaline-producing spots his entire life and he'd never walked away with the feelings like the ones that overwhelmed him now. "Never happened to me before."

FEAR SWAMPED ME.

I'd never had these feelings either. I wanted to embrace them.

What if it *was* just adrenaline?

Except, he felt it too. The inexplicable high from just being near him. The urge to protect, to comfort, to make him laugh, to jump his bones.

His words gave me hope. That hope was like a beacon. A light in the distance showing the way. If that emotion was false, I'd be devastated.

"I wouldn't know. I haven't ever been in a situation like yesterday." I traced his tattoo with my pointer finger. Bent to kiss his biceps and outlined the numbers with my tongue.

Ken nuzzled my neck.

"May 18 keeps popping up," I said cautiously. I knew it was important to him, I just didn't know why.

"My father was one of the protesters killed."

My chest went tight. Words were no comfort. I pressed a kiss to his cheek. Soft. Accepting.

"How old were you?"

"I was a baby. Not yet one."

I was lucky. I'd always had the support of both my parents. Their direction and encouragement helped me achieve everything I wanted.

"It must have been hard on you."

"One cannot miss what one never had."

I couldn't get a bead on whether or not he wanted to keep talking. "Is that when you moved to the US?"

"We didn't move. We fled to California in the middle of the night. My mother feared for our safety so she sought political asylum in the US."

"Wow." I traced his tattoo, waited for him to continue.

"My entire life has been spent in pursuit of the truth about May 18. It has dominated every single act since I was old enough to understand that it was my duty." He said abruptly, "My life was scripted from an early age."

So this was it. I was a footnote in his script. A pleasant

diversion. Which was a normal outcome from a blind date. One night. Then over.

Likely not to be repeated.

"Last night…."

I waited for him to finish, but when he didn't continue I jumped in. "It was a hell of a night." My level of sorrow was not commensurate with the amount of time we'd spent in each other's company. I prepared to kiss him and send him on his way. But the words stuck in my throat and pressure built behind my eyes.

Before I could get the words out, he changed the conversation again. "I've never been in a relationship before."

"Never?"

Why not?

To my surprise, he continued, "I didn't have the luxury of making a connection. I had to stay on task." He cupped my breast in his hand, toyed with my nipple, rubbing his thumb back and forth, seemingly fascinated as my body responded vigorously to his touch.

The answering tingle in my sex was a surprise. I was usually a one-and-done kinda girl. I loved sex but I wasn't a slave to it.

Keep on topic. It was his way of diverting my attention from his confession.

"You found what you've been looking for?" I forced myself to ask.

"I completed my mission," he affirmed.

His mission.

"I know you can't tell me," I began.

"I cannot." His fingers danced over my face, traced the line of my brow, and the curve of my cheek before he tunneled his fingers through my hair and cupped my head.

The gesture was unbelievably tender, sweet.

"Let's just say that I have many allegiances but no master."

I figured that was as close as he'd ever come to admitting that he was a spy, and if I wasn't mistaken, a double spy.

Shit, that was a tough life to live.

I sensed that was where things broke down. "So now what?"

Did he want to continue on missions?

"I...don't know." He bent his head and drew my nipple into his mouth. He tongued the bud with wet, carnal suction reawakening my body in a fierce rush of arousal. I skimmed my hand along his chocolate abs and arrowed toward his erection.

He released my nipple. "I'm finding...I want to live for myself."

"As opposed to?"

"My mother, my countries, my bosses."

"That's a lot of other people." I thought he was telling me that he didn't want another person to answer to.

A sense of loss expanded in my chest pushing out my air, suppressing my ability to breathe. But I consoled myself with the thought that at least we had this short time together.

"My whole life, I've been in darkness," he confessed.

My throat tightened. I wanted to soothe him, but I could only think of a physical response. I wrapped my fingers around his erection. Felt the power and the strength of him in the pulse of his blood. I squeezed, rubbed my palm over the head of his cock.

Got a little lightheaded remembering how he felt inside me. "I've got a short-term solution."

His hair was featherlight against my breastbone. The scruff of his beard scraped against the curve of my breast. I could feel his smile.

"I don't know that I want short term."

My breath caught again. Hope unfurled, stronger than before. I couldn't let him hurt me, even unintentionally. "What exactly are you talking about?"

"You fill me with light."

He rolled onto his back. And with a belly-fluttering

demonstration of his strength, he lifted me up and settled my body on top of his, my legs straddling his hips. His cock brushed my clit, rubbed over the ultra-sensitive nub slick with arousal.

"Oh."

Oh fuck. We needed a condom. Before I could even mention it, he handed me the foil packet.

"You're prepared."

"I always have more than one plan." He slid his hands over my stomach as I lifted up and rolled the condom over his thick erection. His thumbs rubbed over my clit and pressed lightly inside me.

I arched over him, giving him better access. He curled up and captured my breast with his mouth.

And amazingly enough, I was ready again.

My arousal slicked my thighs as he positioned me above him.

I stared down into his eyes as he lowered me onto his erection. His thick length split me in two, breaking me apart and filling me up.

Completing me in a way I'd never felt before.

I rested on his thighs, my ass cradled in his hips. The hair on his legs tickled the backs of mine as I absorbed how amazing he felt inside me.

He began to move, his biceps straining as he lifted and lowered me on his shaft. The angle massaged his cock against my inner walls, and rubbed over my g-spot. The slow, easy pace was in direct contrast to our last frantic bout of lovemaking.

I bent over him, wanting the skin-to-skin contact. My breasts rubbed against his pecs, Our faces were mere inches apart.

I stared into his eyes, the connection between us intense, heated. He gripped my hips, holding on as if I were a life preserver in a roiling sea.

His breath was warm against my lips, and I wanted to kiss him but I didn't want to lose that connection. I was afraid to even blink.

My head went light, as he slowly, reverently rocked us to orgasm. My sex spasmed around his cock.

His gaze went opaque as he emptied into me. His cock pulsed against my ultra-sensitive walls and I quivered with fine tremors. Still I didn't look away. That ephemeral connection shimmered between us, intangible yet undeniable.

I didn't want to break the reverent silence.

"A little more creative," he finally murmured against my neck. His cock was still buried in my pussy. "But still pretty vanilla."

A lightness, a happiness flowed through me at the thoughts of how creative he could get. "How many positions are there in the *Kama Sutra*?"

"Hundreds."

"I guess that means you've got a lot more chances to demonstrate your creativity."

CHAPTER 17

K en woke to a noise so slight, that at first he thought he'd imagined it. No more than a scuff of a heel on the hotel room's entry marble or the brush of bare feet on the lush carpet.

But years of situational awareness, of anticipating attack, had left him with a preternatural sense of danger.

Half on top of him, Barb shifted restlessly in her sleep and he knew their time was up.

He tensed his arms, braced her against him, then rolled them away from the noise, and onto the floor. Just as the whoosh of a hatchet hit the bed.

If he hadn't woken, the thick steel blade would be embedded in his ribs.

His acrobatic move startled Barb. "Ken?" God that soft, breathy word hit him deep in the heart, and he knew in that moment that he wanted to wake to her for the rest of his life.

Of course if he didn't take care of their intruder, this would *be* the rest of his life.

"Stay down on the floor and out of the way," he murmured.

138

Ken hopped to his feet, spread his legs in a fighting stance, arms up and ready.

"Where is it?" The man's voice was gritty, ragged.

The room was dim, only a bit of daylight filtered through the small gap in the blackout curtains.

The fake ambassador stood on the opposite side of the bed. Shoulders hunched, hair askew and coated in a gray ash, he was a complete wreck. But he had that hatchet firmly clenched in his fist again. Fuck. If he threw it, Ken could be seriously injured. Which would leave Barb vulnerable.

"What?"

"Don't play me for stupid," he said. His sunken eyes burned with a killing rage. "Once I discovered that you were the one in the basement bunker, I knew you'd taken the flash drives."

"You know who I am?" Not many managed to surprise Ken but this imposter had.

The fake ambassador laughed harshly until the bark devolved into a fit of hacking coughs. But he didn't answer.

"You have me at a disadvantage." Especially since he was bare-ass naked without a weapon in sight. But he had no fucking clue who the maniac was, or how he'd figured out that Ken would be in Barb's hotel room.

He willed Barb to stay down and out of sight. The guy had to know Barb was here, but Ken was hoping he'd forgotten about her.

"Do you know what it's like to spend your whole life in another's shadow? To spend your whole life labeled by others? Look at Jung-ho, he's the good son, he's the general, he's the ambassador."

This sounded far too personal.

"Trapped by expectation," he ranted. "Jin-ho is the thief, the shady businessman, the profiteer. But Jung-ho, he is the upstanding citizen. He is the son to be proud of."

Right now Ken was trapped between the edge of the bed and

the hotel wall. He needed to maneuver into a more open position.

"Meanwhile, Jung-ho was happy to profit from my business and even contribute. He was the one behind the veil, protected by his status." Crazy swung the hatchet up and back, seemingly mesmerized by the blade. "When in fact, he was the smuggler, the liar, the thief, and I put up with it."

Ken finally understood that this man was Jin-ho, Jung-ho's younger brother, the one he'd never met.

"My whole life I put up with being the second-class citizen, with being the face of the bad son until…."

Ken edged further away from Barb, wanting her removed from the violence about to take place.

"Until what?" Ken watched the guy's eyes, shadowed and tormented, because he was running on emotion. Which meant his eyes would reveal his intent to throw the damn hatchet before he even moved.

"Until I discovered that *my brother*," he spat, "had stolen my son. He'd lied to me for years about *my* son."

"So the boy is yours?" That was twisted.

"He was my son."

Shit. *Was* my son. That past tense was not a good sign.

But Ken didn't want to escalate the situation so he kept his mouth shut.

"We were escaping, away from the house, toward the secret exit. The tunnel was supposed to be reinforced." Jin-ho mourned openly. "Instead, when the house exploded, the tunnel collapsed. A beam hit his chest, crushed him."

Jesus. He couldn't imagine.

"He wasn't even supposed to be there today." Jin-ho's voice broke as he stared down at his hands. In a fit of rage, he whirled, and with a roar, he hurled the hatchet, not at Ken, but at the mirror on the wall.

The glass shattered, shards tinkled to the carpet in muffled thuds. Jin-ho's breath heaved in and out of his chest in thick heavy gasps.

Ken cut his gaze to Barb briefly. She was edging toward the nightstand. He didn't want her moving or drawing any attention to herself but he couldn't acknowledge her actions lest the crazy guy stop talking.

She huddled against the nightstand but she'd taken out her cell and was punching numbers into the keypad on the screen. Thank fuck it was on silent.

Jin-ho turned to face Ken again, his face the very picture of reason, his voice calm. "So you see why I want that flash drive."

In a weird way, Ken could relate to this angry broken man. "I do understand. My whole life I have been tasked with avenging my father's death."

"I know. I know." Jin-ho laughed but not with amusement. "We knew about your obsession. We laughed over it. Because Jung-ho knew you wanted the proof he had. He also knew it would break you."

Ken's stomach roiled with fear. The same things would not break him now. Hopefully Jin-ho had not figured that out.

He raised his gaze to Ken's. "He was just waiting for the right time to use your obsession against you."

Ken thought about the revelations in the files he'd found. The truth about both his birth government and his adopted government and their roles is his father's death. Jung-ho was a smart man. Because that information had tilted his world.

"The long con." Jin-ho broke down laughing but it was a sick, horrified laughter. "He was a pro at it. He conned everyone. Our mother, our country, his wife, me. Everyone."

Sorrow rolled over him in a wave. What the hell did Jin-ho want? Only one way to find out. "So what do you want?"

"I don't want to kill you."

That was a relief. Sort of.

"Or your pretty friend."

Shit. He'd been hoping that Jin-ho had forgotten about Barb.

"But I want that flash drive." His hands clenched, his voice bitter. "I want the world to know about my brother. About his shame."

Ken huffed out a defeated laugh. For years, that had been his only goal. To avenge his father and reveal to the world what had really happened on May 18. Why the peaceful protest had turned into a massacre. "I understand."

He dropped his chin to his chest and breathed slowly.

The temptation to give Jin-ho the file was alluring. To let everyone finally know that his father was not a traitor. That his father had been a patriot until his dying day. He could finally let go of the past.

Except a truth he'd realized, yet not acknowledged, hit him now. Revealing that information would create waves beyond his own personal satisfaction.

In Barb, he saw his future.

Her eyes were wide, her tears gleamed in the low light. The absolute trust in her gaze only confirmed he was making the right decision.

"Then hand it over." Jin-ho demanded. "I will release the information. And the world will know Jung-ho's shame. His guilt."

A strange peace settled over Ken. "I can't let you do that."

The only sound in the room was Jin-ho's breathing. "But this is what you wanted." He sounded completely bewildered.

"I know," Ken replied. "I'm truly sorry."

"No!" Jin-ho rushed Ken.

Ken sidestepped easily. But he knew that the fight wouldn't continue to be easy.

Jin-ho said, "I need that file."

In a series of punches, Jin-ho struck at Ken. He responded with defensive chops.

"I changed my face to make this happen. Had surgery to alter my appearance so I could pass for him."

Jin-ho performed an intricate kata but Ken was able to counter his moves.

"I pretended to be him for days, got the venue of the party changed to the house." His movements became more and more erratic and jerky as he kicked at Ken. "I had sex with the woman who betrayed me. Who took my son into her body and then delivered him to my brother."

Ken didn't want to kill Jin-ho, didn't want another death on his conscience, but he wasn't sure he'd have that luxury. Jin-ho seemed determined that one of them would die and there was no way Ken was losing. He had too much to live for now.

"The only thing I miscalculated was the security for his private room." Jin-ho unleashed a flurry of punches. "Paranoid bastard."

Ken continued to block Jin-ho's movements. "All for revenge?"

"He took and took. I gave and gave. Look where it got me." Devastation washed over his face. And that moment of inattention cost him.

Finally, Ken had Jin-ho in a headlock. All at once, the fight went out of him. He slumped, hung his head to the floor, hands out and open, in classic surrender.

"Do it," Jin-ho begged. "Let me die with honor."

Fuck. That he understood.

Ken grabbed the Karambit from the pocket of his discarded pants.

He heard Barb's soft "oh" but couldn't turn around to reassure her that it would be okay. This was going to create another shit storm. But he'd protect Barb.

"I can't." Ken bowed deeply. Then handed Jin-ho the knife.

Barb flinched as the blade flicked open.

With one sharp, effective plunge, Jin-ho eviscerated himself and fell to the side, never taking his gaze from Ken.

"*Kamsahamnida.*"

Pain and gratitude shone in Jin-ho's eyes as he accepted death.

CHAPTER 18

K en called Carson Black for cleanup. The Sofitel moved them to a new room, while NSA cleaners sanitized Barb's old one.

So many pieces of this clusterfuck would never see a headline. The fact that an imposter had been close enough to the president to shake his hand was front and center. That kind of security lapse could never be exposed.

The details of the terrorist attack on Ambassador Choi's home would be footnotes in a hidden file about a conflict long over but which still had repercussions today. Unfortunately, telling the world would only create more ripples and more unrest. Burying this information was the right thing to do.

Jin-ho would officially die in the blast that killed his brother and his family.

"I understand obsessive need. I also understand that sometimes to be free you need to let go. And when put in a larger perspective, sometimes just knowing the truth is enough." Carson Black tucked the flash drives into his pocket.

Such a small gesture, but the closure was huge. Ken nodded,

unable to put voice to his words. As if she knew how overwhelmed he was, Barb threaded her fingers through his.

Carson smiled at them both. "This is good."

Ken frowned.

"The two of you." Carson wagged his finger between Ken and Barb.

Had Black turned in to some sort of matchmaker now?

"Who would have thought it?" Carson laughed. His bald head gleamed in the sunlight streaming through the sheer curtains. "Jamie's got the touch."

Ken cleared his throat. "One question."

"Perhaps." Carson inclined his head.

"How did you get the code when Jin-ho couldn't?"

He raised one black eyebrow raised and bared his teeth. "Two people had access to that room."

So, Carson's contact must have been the only other person who knew the code. Damn, the man had connections.

By giving Carson the intelligence on the drives, he had cleared his debt to him. "We even?"

"I'll leave you two alone." Carson didn't answer his question. Instead he directed a look at Barb. "Don't be a stranger."

He left as unobtrusively as he'd come.

Barb stared at the closed hotel room door. "Do you think there was an underlying message in that statement?"

A deep amusement bubbled up from his belly. "*Yobo*, there's always an underlying meaning with him."

She blinked as understanding set in. "What does yobo mean?"

"Honey," he said softly. That was what she was. A sweetness, a sharpness he hadn't been looking for but was thrilled to have found.

Barb held his hand with an easy clasp, familiar as if they'd been together for years, not less than twenty-four hours. As if she sensed his conflicted emotions, she said, "Your father would approve."

She was right. His father had been a peaceful protestor, a champion of democracy, and an advocate for a better way of life for his family and his country.

"Releasing that information would destabilize the entire relationship between the Republic of Korea and the United States. It would set diplomatic relations back decades." He tried to shrug it off, but she understood what he'd just done.

She hugged him, taking that burden on. A heavy weight lifted from him.

It was over. Finally over. Instead of dwelling on the past, instead of the constant worry of avenging his father, he was free.

For a moment, that freedom was constricting, confining. What would he do?

And then it hit him. He was free to concentrate on the future. In all its forms. And he knew exactly who he wanted to concentrate on.

"I'm free."

FREE.

"What?" My heart rate accelerated.

"I'm free," he said it again, a great big grin on his face and his dimples peeking out.

"Ah." My shoulders slumped, he no longer had to answer to anyone. Well, it had been fun while it lasted. "That's…great."

It was stupid to be this disappointed. We'd known each other less than one day. That connection I thought we had was probably nothing. I forced a smile, determined to be happy for him.

"Free to concentrate on the future."

I squeezed his hand, savored that last physical connection

between us, the solidness of his palm against mine, then tried to disentangle our fingers. "Congratulations."

But he wasn't letting go. "You want to get a late breakfast?" Ken played with my fingers.

I was oddly hesitant. On one hand, I wanted to close this date out. Get on with life. On the other hand, I hated to let him walk away. Because I'd figured out I didn't need a baby or a bunch of adventures on a bucket list. Just him.

A queer hope blossomed in me. I didn't need to wait around for him to ask me.

Before I could tell him what I wanted, *him*, he curled his arms around my waist and pulled me close.

"Fuck it. Who needs food? We can subsist on sex alone for another few days."

Of course we could.

"Was that you…asking me out on a date?"

"Sure."

A date? I think we were a little further along than a date. Not to mention, our first date didn't go so well. "I don't know if I want to date you."

He eyed me, trying to figure out if I was serious.

I complained. Sort of. "For our first date, we were almost taken hostage, shot at, and blown up."

"Best first date ever," Ken replied with a stoic face.

Hell yes, it was. Epic.

"For our second date, we were almost killed by a hatchet-wielding imposter." I shuddered, less inclined to make a joke about Jin-ho.

Jin-ho's sacrifice was tragic. Ken had been able to relate to him. I wanted to make sure he didn't suffer the same fate. I wanted to make him happy. Make him show me those dimples.

"Second date is always a litmus test," he said.

Jesus, he thought our relationship was a harbinger of death and destruction? "It was a serious low point," I countered.

"Only place to go is up."

That was for damn sure.

Ken pressed a chaste kiss to my forehead. My forehead? Maybe that was his way of backing off. He felt guilty.

"Think of the awesome story this will make for our grandchildren."

I stilled. Grandchildren? My whole body shimmied. Yesterday, he hadn't even considered the possibility of children.

That was moving too fast.

Except I felt it too. I leaned my head on his shoulder. "What did I ever do in a former life to deserve you?"

"Pretty sure we deserve each other."

I raised an eyebrow.

"Let's consider breakfast our third date." Ken said, "Food. Mimosas. Sex."

I could get on board with that.

He nuzzled my neck, kissed his way across my collarbone. Then, he clinched it. "Of course, all I need is you."

I melted. "Yes. I would be honored to go on a date with you." I snuggled closer, needing his touch. Needing him.

"After all," I started and Ken finished, "Third time's a charm."

THANK you for reading Barb and Ken's story!! I hope you enjoyed reading this story as much as I enjoyed writing it! There were several inspirations for this novel. I regularly re-watch Die Hard. Such a fantastic movie. And then I fell in love with Korean action-adventure movies while doing research for Ken and his story. So much tragedy! Of course, I wanted a romance too and I knew that Barb needed an extraordinary story.

If you did enjoy this book, below are a few ways you can help a writer out!!

. . .

GOOD: Lend the book to a friend

BETTER: Recommend the book to your friends

BEST: Leave a review at Amazon, BN, Goodreads, Apple, Kobo…basically any place they sell or review eBooks. Every review helps my work get out to other readers and I cannot even express how much it means to me when you let people know you liked my work. Readers have so many choices nowadays and limited dollars to spend. It can be difficult to take a chance on a new author even if the premise sounds appealing. By reviewing books, you give other readers insight into the story world and help them make informed purchases.

THANK YOU, thank you, thank you for your support!!

P.S. Would you like to know when my next book is available? You can sign up for my new release email list/newsletter at Lisa's Confidants.

My newsletter sign up also includes a link to the free short story of when Jamie and Lucas met.

AUTHOR'S NOTE AND ACKNOWLEDGMENTS

I had an absolute blast writing this book and learning more about Korean culture.

The Gwangju Uprising is an actual event and there are still questions surrounding what really happened regarding the actions of both the Republic of Korea and the United States governments. The Korean government swears that the initial violence was an accident. I took the liberty of instituting my own suppositions about what happened.

For more information on the Korean door carvings visit: http://koreatourinformation.com/blog/2013/12/06/beautiful-museum-for-traditional-windows-and-doors-chungwonsanbang-master/

If you want to see some of the photo inspirations for the Korean details in the book, visit my pinterest story board: https://www.pinterest.com/lisahugheyautho/dangerous-games-black-cipher-files-4/

Much thanks to all the usual suspects. A giant thanks to Deb Nemeth for being flexible when my computer ate my homework. LOL.

And to my most awesome friend Martha whose love of Die Hard exceeds my own.

EXCERPT FROM BLOWBACK

Blowback (blo′ bak) *n.* A deadly, unintended consequence of a covert operation.

Eerie blue light penetrated my consciousness first. The regulated thump-thump of tires pounded in my head, echoing with fierce resonance.

Where the hell was I? Why did I feel like this? I kept my eyes closed, knowing pretense was paramount to my survival. Wherever I was, it wasn't normal.

Ha. My life would never be normal.

I tracked back to my last memory. I'd hooked up with a guy. Had relatively indiscriminate sex with him.

I inhaled shallowly, carefully, not wanting to give away anything. I still smelled like sex. Really great sex.

I wanted to smile but kept my expression lax.

I'd longed to stay in that bed. Sleep with him. Just sleep with the comforting warmth of another human being. The ache had been so intense that as soon as he dozed off--I left.

That was my last memory.

"You can stop pretending."

I continued to fake sleep. I didn't know that male voice. It was bland, not angry, but with a slight smirk, as if he knew something I didn't.

"You should be awake by now. We calibrate our doses very carefully."

That statement raised so many questions, I decided to comply with his unspoken request and let my eyes drift open. I calculated we were moving at a speed of about thirty miles per hour. Suburban, blacked out windows, bulletproof glass. The blue light came from the interior dome in the big SUV.

"The light is to protect your eyes. The drug affects your pupil's ability to dilate and contract."

What drug? I kept silent.

"Not very curious, are you?"

My last conscious memory was from the motel off of 295 near Alexandria around nine in the evening. It was pitch dark out now, so I'd been out for a while.

Lucas. Could the guy have been a plant? Possible. Since he was my last clear memory, it made sense.

I sifted through the spaghetti of my brain. For the past two days, I'd been undercover, shadowing Staci Grant's life. Last night, I'd encountered Lucas Goodman, who'd been looking for Staci and thought he'd found her when he found me. The sexual heat between us had been instantaneous and mutual. A few sweaty hours later, I'd left, confident my movements as Staci had been tracked. My cover had been working.

They'd kidnapped Staci.

Excellent.

I was right where I needed to be.

Now I needed answers. My task was to discover why CIA, DIA, and NSA agents were being kidnapped, the method of interrogation, and who was doing the kidnapping. The answers would be coming. I just had to be ready.

I settled into the backseat of the car to wait, taking in details.

Mistake number one. They hadn't taken my ring, so the satellite audio transmitter should work. I twisted the unusual ring with my thumb and pressed the citrine stone twice. I was now sending voice-activated recordings back to Carson.

Mistake number two. They'd cuffed my hands, in front, but left my legs unshackled.

They'd taken my government firearm but missed the knife in the sheath at my waist. Mistake number three. Always, always check everywhere for hidden weapons.

Although my mind was the most powerful weapon I had.

My watch was gone and my government-issue GPS with it. Slouching to the side, I got a better view of the dashboard panel. My kidnapper had conveniently supplied me with another GPS system, live and tracking.

Coordinates. Latitude–47. Longitude–122. I was in the Pacific Northwest. I looked out the misted window to see a reflection of the Space Needle and pinpointed my location as Seattle. I was a long way from Virginia.

I returned my gaze to the kidnapper. Subject was male, small head, blond hair gelled into little spikes, crescent-shaped birthmark below his right ear.

The car rolled to a stop. The rocking intensified my queasy stomach. I ignored it.

"We're here."

Here was a warehouse near the water. The guy wasn't rough but the sudden motion as he lugged me out of the SUV caused my stomach to roil.

I breathed in the cold, damp air through my nose, trying to quell the nausea. As he led me toward a semi-truck trailer, I noted the parking lot was empty except for one other truck and a car, too far away and too dark to make out details. The warehouse, constructed with long cinder block walls interrupted by doors at twenty foot intervals, was to my left and behind me.

The trailer was modified from a regular shipping container,

doors locked up tight in the back, with another entrance on the side. It looked as if the stairs were all one solid block which could fold up into the interior of the trailer.

The recessed entrance looked exactly like an old-fashioned front door complete with screen door. A porch light flicked on. The screen door wheezed open as a dark-haired woman in a white coat stepped out onto the platform.

The light behind her filled the doorway with shadows. I couldn't make out her features but I caught a furtive movement, the light illuminating her hand as she tucked a syringe into her pocket.

"Thank you. You can go now." She nodded regally to the man holding me. Her melodic voice held a hint of Asia, probably second-generation American.

He promptly let go of my arm and walked away. They must believe that the plastic restraint cuffs would be a big deterrent to resistance. The click of his heels echoed in the silence as she stared at me, her hands clasped tightly in front of her, so tightly her knuckles showed white.

There was something in her stance--tension, stress? I eased back a step.

"Welcome." She put a hand on the railing and took a step down. Then she hesitated and glanced back at the open doorway. "We won't hurt you."

I thought about the syringe in her pocket. *No thank you.*

I'd had drug resistance training but honestly I didn't want to put it to the test. At least, not yet. Although if that scenario became unavoidable and they pumped me full of drugs, the transmitter in my ring guaranteed I would get the information Carson and the NSA needed.

All of the kidnapped agents had an unidentified drug in their bloodstream and unknown consequences from those drugs. We had no idea what national secrets they'd given away or what kind of long-term effects were possible from the drug cocktail most likely in that syringe. My job was to get myself kidnapped, acquire the drugs, identify the perpetrators, and get out before they could accomplish their objective.

I wobbled as if unsteady on my feet and eased back two steps, assessing my position.

As the Suburban left, the beam from the head lamps shone on her. The shape of her face and the tilt of her eyes marked her as Chinese. Lines of strain curled around her mouth, the expression was supposed to be a smile but came off as more of a grimace. "Come with me."

I don't think so.

I'd expected the kidnapping, the intel suggested that Staci Grant would be next. I'd planned to resist at first. I didn't want to make it too easy for them to subdue me. Carson was supposed to have a team on standby waiting to capture the kidnappers after I completed my objectives. But since we hadn't planned for a cross country abduction–all of the other kidnappings had been local and accomplished within a matter of several hours–it would most likely take a little time before the extraction team got here.

If they got here.

I pivoted and ran for the warehouse door nearest me. Her footsteps rang on the metal steps as she followed.

"She's getting away." A man's shout, older, deeper, slightly frantic, registered as I reached the door. Two against one. More difficult, but not impossible. Woman, older man. Until I saw his physique, I couldn't judge who was more dangerous.

"I've got it," the woman replied and sprinted toward me.

I yanked on the handle, flung the door open, and slid inside. The heavy metal swung shut with an ominous clang.

Obviously, the drugs were making me melodramatic.

The warehouse was dimly lit. Industrial metal lights hung from the ceiling, their muted pink glow making the surroundings blurry. Metal shelving separated the concrete floor into long, wide aisles. Three tiers of jumbo shelves housed wooden pallets of goods. I stood at the end of one aisle.

I hustled over two aisles, pulling the knife from the sheath at my waist as I went. The restraint cuffs at my wrists took a few swipes before slicing clean through.

I grabbed some small ceramic rice bowls and shoved them into my jacket pockets. Mistake number four. They'd let me keep my jacket.

The door banged open.

"Don't let her escape." I could hear the man huffing, and a rhythmic thumping noise as they pursued.

"She won't escape," the woman replied grimly from somewhere behind me.

I stalked down the industrial cement aisle, my footsteps silent. Glancing around, I searched for another way out.

"Please don't try to escape, Agent Hunt." The man's plea had a desperate edge to it.

My legs faltered. I wanted to stop, stand rooted to the floor. Only training kept me moving.

He'd spoken my real name. My *real* name, not the cover I was using for this assignment. So who did they really want?

Me, Jamie Hunt, NSA agent? Or Staci Grant, CIA officer?

KOREAN TERMS

Yobo = honey
   Ju-seyo = please
   Kamsahamnida = thank you
   Chagiya = darling
   Jen-jang = shit
   Shi-bal = fuck
   Gaejasik = motherfucker

ABOUT LISA

USA Today Bestselling Author Lisa Hughey started writing romance in the fourth grade. That particular story involved a prince and an engagement. Now, she writes about strong heroines who are perfectly capable of rescuing themselves and the heroes who love both their strength and their vulnerability. She pens romances of all types—suspense, paranormal, and contemporary—but at their heart, all her books celebrate the power of love.

She lives in Cape Ann Massachusetts with her fabulously supportive husband, two out of three awesome mostly-grown kids, and one somewhat grumpy cat.

Beach walks, hiking, and traveling are her favorite ways to pass the time when she isn't plotting new ways to get her characters to fall in love.

Lisa loves to hear from readers and has tons of places you can connect with her. It's a wonder she gets any writing done at all....

Be Lisa's Friend on Facebook

Follow Lisa on Twitter
Become a member of Lisa's Confidants
Visit Lisa on the Web
Follow Lisa on Pinterest
Follow Lisa on Instagram
Email Lisa
Be Lisa's Friend on Goodreads
Like Lisa on Facebook at Lisa Hughey Author

ALSO BY LISA HUGHEY

Black Cipher Files Romantic Suspense

The Encounter, A Prequel to Blowback

Blowback

Betrayals

Burned

Dangerous Game

**These books are also available in paperback

Black Cipher Files Box Set (includes Blowback, Betrayals, and Burned)

Snow Creek Christmas

Love on Main Street: A Snow Creek Christmas – 7 Author anthology

One Silent Night (from Love on Main Street)

Miracle on Main Street (standalone novella)

Family Stone Romantic Suspense

Stone Cold Heart, (Jess, Family Stone #1)

Carved in Stone (Connor, Family Stone #2)

Heart of Stone (Riley, Family Stone #3)

Still the One (Jack, Family Stone #4)

Jar of Hearts (Keisha & Shane, Family Stone #5)

Queen of Hearts (Shelley, Family Stone #6)

Cold as Stone (John, Family Stone #7)

Family Stone Box Set (Stone Cold Heart, Carved in Stone, Heart of

Stone, Still the One, & Jar of Hearts)

The Nostradamus Prophecies

View To A Kill #1

Never Say Never #2

ALIAS

Stalked (ALIAS #1)

Hunted (ALIAS #2)

Vanished (ALIAS #3)

Saved (ALIAS #3.5)

Deceived (ALIAS #4)

Billionaire Breakfast Club

His Semi-Charmed Life (Camp Firefly Falls #11 and Billionaire Breakfast Club #0)

Everything He Wants (Billionaire Breakfast Club #1 The Jock)

Queen of His Daydreams (Camp Firefly Falls #23 and Billionaire Breakfast Club #1.5)

BLACK CIPHER FILES SERIES

The Black Cipher Files is a fast-paced, edgy romance and espionage series that features hot, alpha heroes and kick-ass heroines, working to uncover long-buried secrets from the past so they can save their future.

BLOWBACK

Years ago, Jamie Hunt sacrificed everything to keep her sister protected and safe. Now she lives alone, works alone, survives alone. When a covert mission goes horribly wrong, she can trust no one.

On the trail of a missing teenager, private investigator Lucas Goodman's investigation leads him to Jamie. Despite her attempts to ditch him, Lucas tenaciously shadows Jamie, realizing he doesn't just want information...he wants her.

When Jamie's sister is in danger, Jamie is forced to team up with Lucas. Together they must expose the connection between agents' murders, a missing teenager, and a sixty-year-old government conspiracy.

BETRAYALS

Staci Grant is dead. Jordan Ramirez saw the photographs, but he refuses to believe. His missing lover is the best CIA officer in the field. Now Jordan must find Staci and convince her that trusting him means the difference between staying alive or staying dead.

Staci has been betrayed. Captured, imprisoned and tortured, it took all her skills to escape. Now she is determined to uncover who set her up and why, a mission that leaves no room for trust.

When Jordan finds her, he won't take no for an answer, and together they desperately race to unravel a decades' old secret. But each revelation brings fresh betrayals that threaten their love and their lives.

BURNED

Zeke Hawthorne, a programmer and hacker at the NSA, is in trouble. Under investigation to make sure had hasn't divulged national secrets, he's sent on a boondoggle. All he has to do is keep an eye on Sunshine, from afar, and make sure she's safe.

Sunshine Smith's entire world was blown apart thirteen years ago when her obsessive stepfather killed her grandparents. She and her mother went into hiding to escape. For years they've been safe...until now.

When Sunshine is threatened, Zeke cannot keep his distance. Only danger and betrayal are coming for Zeke too. Zeke and Sunshine must combine forces to stay one step ahead of the peril that stalks them, but trust between two people who grew up without faith is a difficult bond to form.